THE DIVAS: AALIYAH

Other books in The Divas series
by Victoria Christopher Murray

Diamond
India
Veronique

THE DIVAS:
AALIYAH

Victoria Christopher Murray

POCKET BOOKS
New York   London   Toronto   Sydney

Pocket Books
A Division of Simon & Schuster, Inc.
1230 Avenue of the Americas
New York, NY 10020

First Pocket Books trade paperback edition October 2009

POCKET and colophon are registered trademarks of Simon & Schuster, Inc.

For information about special discounts for bulk purchases,
please contact Simon & Schuster Special Sales at 1-866-506-1949
or business@simonandschuster.com.

The Simon & Schuster Speakers Bureau can bring authors to your
live event. For more information or to book an event contact the
Simon & Schuster Speakers Bureau at 1-866-248-3049 or visit our
website at www.simonspeakers.com.

Manufactured in the United States of America

10   9   8   7   6   5   4   3   2   1

Library of Congress Cataloging-in-Publication Data

Murray, Victoria Christopher.
  Aaliyah / by Victoria Christopher Murray.
    p. cm. — (Divas)
  Summary: The Divine Divas are elated to reach the Glory 2 God Teen Talent
Search finals, but then Aaliyah learns that her mother, the singing sensation
Zena, will be the group's mentor, and she must figure out how to tell her best
friends that she lied about her mother being dead.
  1. Mothers and daughters—Fiction. 2. Singers—Fiction. 3. Gospel music—
Fiction. 4. Best friends—Fiction. 5. Friendship—Fiction.
  6. African Americans—Fiction. I. Title.
  PZ7 .M9663Aa1 2009
  [Fic]—dc22   2009009536

ISBN 978-1-4165-6351-8

THE DIVAS: AALIYAH

 # Chapter 1

I was about to have a straight-up heart attack!

For real—not one of those fake ones that my girl Diamond was always having. The way my heart was pounding inside my chest, I was gonna pass out for sure.

When I looked over at my girls, I could tell they felt the exact same way. My best friend for life, India, was standing so still, just grinning like she was in shock. And Veronique looked like she was going to faint from happiness, though I wasn't sure if she was all excited about the Divine Divas or about Arjay Lennox, who had stayed right by her side ever since we ran off the stage.

The only one who was standing like this was no big deal was Diamond—our leader, or at least that's what *she* thought. Yeah, Diamond was just standing with her arms folded—like she knew all along that the Divine Divas were going to make it to the finals of the Glory 2 God Teen Talent Search.

I mean, I had a lot of confidence, trust that. But no one in the world had more confidence than Diamond. It's not that I didn't think we could sing; every single one of my girls could carry at least half a tune. But when we started this whole thing back in September, I never would've believed that we would have made it all the way to the finals. All the way to Miami—South Beach, to be exact. We would be competing with four other groups.

But I wasn't hardly worried—I knew for sure that my girls and I were going to shut this whole thing down. At the end, we were gonna be the ones with the recording contract.

Just thinking about that made my heart start crashing again. Could this really happen? Could the Divine Divas really get a $250,000 recording contract and move into the big time?

Not that I was sure that this was the way I wanted it to go down. I mean, I was into winning, don't sleep. But I wasn't about to give up any part of my dreams. No way. No matter what happened with my girls and the Divine Divas, in two years, I was going to Harvard. Trust that. And, I was going to become a nuclear physicist. You could bank on that, too. If we won this thing, we'd just have to find a way to work it out.

"Hey, what you doing over here all by yourself, Pretty Lady?"

I had to lean my head all the way back to look up at Troy. He was that tall and one of the Three Ys Men, who were our backup dancers. The way he was grinning in my face, I could tell he was as happy as we were. I guess this whole winning thing was as exciting for the guys as it was for us, even though we were the ones who were out front.

"I'm not doing anything." I tried to shrug Troy off, but it was hard. I could tell by the way Troy had been looking at me ever since we got to New York that he kinda liked me, but I didn't know for sure. It could've been that he just wanted to hang with me because his boys—Riley and Arjay—had already hooked up with India and Veronique.

But it didn't matter—I liked Troy; I just didn't like him like that. Not that I wasn't into guys; I mean, Troy was major fine. But I had a plan for my life. And right about now, boys—even cute ones—just didn't fit in.

"So, Aaliyah, ah—"

"Hey, baby girl!"

Whew! I was so glad my dad came over and interrupted Troy. I could tell he was going to do something like ask me if I wanted to go out with him when we got back to Los Angeles.

"Hey, Daddy," I said, hugging my father. He was the only male I was into impressing right about now.

"I'm so proud of you," my dad said. He looked at Troy and added, "I'm proud of all of you. You guys were fierce."

"Daddy, *nobody* says *fierce* anymore."

My dad frowned. "Nobody?"

I shook my head. "Only Diamond and Tyra."

"Well, if it's good enough for Diamond and Tyra, it's good enough for me."

Troy and I laughed with my dad, but then we stopped when Roberto Hamilton, the president of Glory 2 God Productions, came into the room where we were hanging out.

"Thank you for waiting," Mr. Roberto said. "And congratulations, once again, to all of you."

As Mr. Roberto looked around the room, I did, too. Even though we were in New York, this room was filled with people from our church in Los Angeles. Besides me and my girls, and the Three Ys Men and our parents (except for Veronique—her mom, Ms. Lena, never came to any of the competitions), there was Pastor Ford and her crew. And about twenty other people from Hope Chapel packing this place.

But when everybody was as happy as we were, it didn't matter if we were standing so close it felt like we were in a club or something.

3

"Well." Mr. Roberto's voice made me turn back to him as he said, "We are at the final round. How do you feel?"

He was just talking to me and my girls, but a whole bunch of people answered, "Great," "Just fine," "All right!" as if they were the ones who had been doing all the singing.

Mr. Roberto laughed. "So, now that we're here, we wanted to let you know just how seriously we're taking this whole competition."

I took a deep breath.

"We're looking for the next big group."

I couldn't help but grin, and my girls were cheesin', too.

"And on the G2G label, that means that we're looking for young men and women who'll be able to perform at the highest levels."

Okay, I thought. That was certainly us. I mean, we were the Divine Divas. We were . . . *fierce*. I grinned as I thought about what I'd just told my father.

"Sometimes you're going to have to perform under pressure, sometimes you're going to have to perform on short notice, you're going to have to perform with big names, all kinds of things."

I wasn't a nuclear physicist yet, but I didn't have to be one to know that Mr. Roberto was building up to something big. I guess this competition really was straight serious now.

"So because of that, we've decided to give each of the remaining groups a mentor."

Diamond was already clapping her hands like she knew what Mr. Roberto was talking about.

"You're going to be working with someone who's already been through all of this," he continued.

"Oh, my God," Diamond yelled out. She held her hand to her chest like she was going to have a heart attack.

Even though India and Veronique rolled their eyes while

Diamond went all the way to her dramatic side, I couldn't hate. I mean, five minutes ago I was having my own heart attack.

"I know who it is!" Diamond shouted out and raised her hand like we were in class or something. Now *that* was funny. 'Cause Diamond was in my chemistry class, and she never raised her hand for anything!

"You think you know?" Mr. Roberto grinned.

"Uh-huh!" Diamond nodded. "It's . . . Yolanda Adams!" And then she snapped her fingers in the air like she had nailed it.

The way Mr. Roberto shook his head and Diamond pouted and frowned like she was confused made everybody laugh.

Mr. Roberto said, "I'm not going to stand here and make you guess. Let me introduce all of you to the mentor for the Divine Divas." Then he stopped, like he was waiting for a drumroll.

He turned toward the door and I peeked around my dad. All kinds of people were going through my head: Beyoncé, Mariah . . . oh, oh, I know. I just loved Rihanna!

And then she walked into the room.

"Ladies and gentlemen, let me introduce . . . Zena!"

"Oh, my God!"

It was Diamond screaming, but now I was the one having a heart attack. For real!

I couldn't breathe. I couldn't think. I pushed my hand against my chest, 'cause I was sure my heart was going to poke right through my skin.

Then, my knees . . . I don't know what happened. But they got rubbery.

By the time I dropped to the floor, I couldn't hear or see a thing.

Chapter 2

My head was hurting really bad.

I opened my eyes and looked straight into my father's face. His eyebrows were bunched together like he was worried or scared or something.

When I tried to lift up my head, he said, "No, no. Stay still, sweetheart." He brushed my braids away from my face. "The ambulance is on its way."

Ambulance? Why did I need any ambulance? And why was I stretched out like this on the floor?

Behind my head, I could hear people walking around and talking all fast. And then I thought I heard Diamond. Yeah . . . it was Diamond, because she was the only one I knew who screeched like that.

"What's wrong with her?" That's what Diamond was screaming over and over and over.

Was she talking about me? There was nothing wrong with me, and I needed to let my girls know that. I tried to sit up again, but then I really felt it. Only this time, it wasn't my head that was hurting. This time, I hurt because I remembered what had happened.

I lay back down, even though I really did feel fine. I didn't need any ambulance. I just needed for my dad to tell me what was going on.

"Dad, why did he . . . is it . . ." I couldn't even finish my sentences.

But I didn't have to. My dad started nodding his head like he knew what I was going to say. That happened a lot with my father and me. He always knew what I was thinking. Sometimes I thought it was because he and I spent so much time together. But truth—my dad had mad skills; there was a reason why he was the assistant chief of police and Diamond called him Top Cop.

"Daddy, why didn't you tell me?" I hated the way I sounded. Kinda like Diamond when she got upset, all whiney and screechy.

He shook his head again. "Ssshhh. Don't try to talk. Everything's going to be fine."

How could he say that? Nothing was going to be fine ever again. I could feel someone walking really close to me, and my heart started doing that hard beating thing. I squeezed my eyes closed—as tight as I could.

Please God. Don't let it be Zena.

I said Amen to myself, then peeked through one eye. And I was so happy when I saw Pastor Ford leaning over me. She didn't say anything; all she did was take my hand and nod her head.

Okay, it didn't take a nuclear physicist to figure out that she knew what was going down. My dad had probably told her everything. Or maybe he hadn't said a word and Pastor Ford had figured it out on her own. She was special like that. She had this serious thing going on with God where she knew everything; she'd probably known about Zena all along.

But then that couldn't be true, because if Pastor Ford had known all this time, she wouldn't have let me tell that big ole lie for so long. She never would have let me tell my girls that my mother was dead.

Oh, brother! How was I going to get out of this? How was I going to tell my girls that I had lied to them ever since we were in the third grade? How was I going to say that my mother wasn't dead; that she was the superstar Zena?

This was going to be some straight-up mad mess.

That was the last thing I thought about before a whole bunch of paramedics came crashing into the room.

Chapter 3

It felt like I was walking inside a fog.

My eyes opened up and all I could see was white and light. But it didn't take any time for me to figure it out—I was in the hospital just waking up from that shot one of those guys in the ambulance had given me.

I wanted to get up and out of there, but then I heard the whispers. When I turned my head just a little, I saw them, and I shut my eyes real fast.

I was hoping they hadn't seen me; and the way they kept going at it, I knew they hadn't.

It's not like I could say that I remembered all that much about my mother. There were little things inside my head—like Zena reading to me before I went to bed. Or singing special songs that she made up with my name. But truth—I don't know if I really remembered that stuff or if it was just in my head because of the things my dad had told me.

But if there was one thing I did know, it was her voice.

And right now her voice sounded just like I'd known it would. Just like it sounded in my dreams.

I squeezed my eyes tighter and tried to open my ears wider so that I could hear what they were whispering about.

"So, what did you expect?" my dad said.

"I . . . didn't know what else to do." Her talking voice sounded just like her singing voice—only better.

My dad said, "You shouldn't have come back, not this way."

"And how many ways were there to do this, Heber? I knew that if I called, you would've never let me see her."

"That's what we agreed; that was your decision."

Then there was quiet.

Uh-oh, I thought. I could feel it—first my dad's eyes. Then I heard his footsteps coming closer to the bed. I figured he was guessing that I was awake, that I was listening. Like I said, they didn't call him Top Cop for nothing.

But there was a reason why my girls called me Top Cop, Junior. 'Cause I had skills, too. Even though I could feel my father real close, I just lay still, like I was a statue. For like a minute, there wasn't any kind of sound. Then after a while, I felt him walk away before the door to the room opened and closed.

I waited for just a little while longer before I peeked out of one eye. *Dang!* They were gone. I had wanted to hear more. I'd wanted to hear my dad tell Zena off; and then tell her to go away and to do what she'd been doing—staying away from me and Los Angeles.

But truth—I guess the way my dad did this was cool. Taking her out of the room meant that I wouldn't have to see her up close, wouldn't have to talk to her at all.

Yeah, the more I thought about it, the better it was. There was no need for me to see Zena. Or talk to her. My dad wouldn't let her come back, and that was a good thing, 'cause I didn't want her in my life anyway.

Chapter 4

I don't think there was ever a time I was so glad to see my girls. Even when Diamond ran in and fell across my bed all dramatic, I couldn't hate.

"I am soooo glad that you're okay!" Diamond sounded like she was about to cry.

"Yeah," India said in her regular soft voice. "We were really worried when you fainted."

Veronique didn't say a word. All she did was sit on the edge of the bed and hold my hand. India came around to the other side, but Diamond stayed right where she was—flung across the bottom of my bed looking like if she stood up, *she* would faint and the doctors would have to come and take her away.

"No worries; I'm okay, you guys." I pushed myself up so that they could see that even though they had me wearing one of those crazy paper robes, I was fine.

"But you fainted," Diamond whined. "You can't *possibly* be all right."

I almost laughed. My girl was talking like she was acting in a movie or something.

"Yeah, like when I fainted," India piped in.

"But you were really sick," I told her. "I'm not; the doctor said that my blood pressure got a little high, and he gave me something to calm down."

"Blood pressure?" Diamond said those words as if she didn't understand. "Isn't that something that old people get?"

I rolled my eyes. The one thing we could always count on was for Diamond to say something absolutely absurd. "We all have blood pressure, Diamond. Mine was just higher than it was supposed to be."

Still lying across the bed, Diamond said, "That's what I'm talking about. You're a teenager; why would you have high blood pressure?"

"The doctor said it was because I got upset." I really didn't want to say anything else, but the way my girls were looking at me, I knew they were waiting for more. Even India's eyes were opened wide. So I added, "It was just that. . . ." My voice got softer, and I couldn't look at them. "I was a little . . . surprised."

That got Diamond moving. She popped up from my bed and almost knocked India down when she pushed her aside. Leaning on the bed rail, Diamond looked me straight in my eyes. "Surprised? Is that what you call it? Girlfriend, you'd better give it up. So"—she paused for a moment—"your mother is. . . ."

Diamond stopped right there, as if she needed me to finish the sentence for her.

At this point, I didn't know what my girls had heard, but the way their eyes were all wide and waiting, they knew something. There was nothing I could do now but tell the God's honest truth. I just hoped they wouldn't be mad at me. I took a deep breath. "Zena is my mother."

Diamond's head fell back and she howled, shocking the heck out of all of us. I couldn't tell if she was crying or laughing.

Veronique put her hand over Diamond's mouth and growled, "If you do that again, they're going to make us leave."

Diamond nodded; she wasn't about to get kicked out of my hospital room. Not now. Not when she was on the verge of hearing the whole story, because if there was one thing about Diamond, she wasn't going to miss out on some good gossip. Diamond was nothing but straight-up drama.

When Veronique took her hand away from Diamond's face, she started talking right away. "Is Zena really your mom?" But Diamond didn't even give me a chance to answer. "Dang, I heard my mom talking—well, she didn't know I was listening—but I thought I'd heard wrong or that she was confused or something." She stared at me as if she wasn't sure if I was telling the truth. "But you told us that Zena was dead."

I shook my head. "I never said Zena was dead. I said my mother was dead."

The looks on their faces let me know that they didn't see the difference. But there was a humongous difference to me; I just didn't know how to explain it to them.

Diamond said, "Zena . . . your mom . . . it's the same person."

She was the one doing all the talking, but I could tell that India and Veronique were thinking the same thing.

I shrugged. "It's a long story."

"If she was my mother," Diamond kept on like she was the spokesperson, "y'all would have known about it from the jump. I would've been shouting it from the roof." She stopped and looked at me kinda sideways. "We're your crew; when you roll, we roll. So why didn't you tell us?"

"Diamond," India began, "I can't believe you're trying to

get all up in Aaliyah's business right now. I mean, look where we are." India spread her arms wide. "She's in the hospital," she said in a way that was supposed to make Diamond shut up.

See, that's why India was my BFFL. Don't get me wrong—I loved me some Diamond and Veronique, too, but it was different with India. She got me. Sometimes I didn't even have to say a word and India would understand. She understood things I didn't understand myself.

India said, "We should just let Aaliyah rest. We can talk about this later." Everybody always said I was the mature one, but India sounded like the most mature one right about now.

Veronique said, "Yeah," but Diamond wasn't about to let it go.

She crossed her arms and frowned as she looked straight at me. "I thought you said you were fine." She didn't even give me time to answer before she was moving her hands in the air like she wanted me to just get on with my story. "High blood pressure doesn't stop you from talking."

At any other time, this is where I would have told Diamond to just be quiet. But I couldn't hate. I mean, if I were in her place, I would be asking the same questions. We were all like sisters, and I had lied to them our whole lives.

Before I had the chance to figure out what to say, my dad walked in. Top Cop to my rescue, for real.

"Ladies, I hate to break this up, but you all have to get going. You still have to go back to the hotel and get your things before you head to the airport."

"I thought we missed our flight," Diamond said.

My dad answered, "We got you on the last one out of New York tonight."

"Oh, dang! I was hoping that since Aaliyah fainted, we would stay another day and I could do some more shopping."

I wasn't the only one who looked at Diamond like she was out of her mind. Leave it to her to turn my disaster into something all about her.

India rolled her eyes at Diamond before she looked at my father, then at me, then back at my father. "What about Aaliyah?" To me, India asked, "You're not coming with us?"

I shrugged. I didn't know what was going on.

"We're taking a flight back in the morning," my father explained. "The doctors just want to make sure my baby girl's okay before they send her twenty thousand feet into the air."

My girls looked all sad, like they were afraid if they left me now, they might never see me again. "I'm fine," I said, trying to make them feel better. "I'll see you tomorrow when I get back."

The way they hugged me almost made me want to cry. Made me want to tell my dad that I just had to be on the plane with them. But there was no talking to my father about this kind of stuff. I was in the hospital, and to him this was serious. And when stuff got serious, my dad stepped up. He was in charge.

"We'll see you tomorrow," India said.

Veronique said, "Yeah, peace out."

"And oh," India added, "the guys said to tell you to get better quick."

"Yeah," Diamond laughed a little. "Troy said to tell you to be easy."

My girls walked so slowly that it felt like it took five minutes before I was alone with my dad.

I said, "I really feel fine, Daddy," thinking that maybe with just a little push, he might let me get on the plane with my girls.

He shook his head. "I'm glad you're feeling better, but we're not taking any chances."

"Do I have to spend the night here?"

"No. We're going back to the hotel. The doctor's going to

check your pressure in an hour or so. He'll probably release you then."

I let out a long breath. That was good. Not that I was a baby or anything; I just didn't want to stay in this hospital by myself. But knowing my dad, he would have pulled up a chair and stayed with me all night.

"There is one other thing," my dad said.

Uh-oh. I didn't like the way he sounded. What was up? Was I sicker than I thought?

"It's Zena." He stopped as if he wanted to make sure I recognized her name. "She wants to see you."

I was shaking my head no before he even finished. "I thought you told her that she couldn't see me," I blurted out, and as soon as those words came out of my mouth, I was sorry. I had given myself up.

My father smiled just a little, but I didn't. There was nothing funny about what he was asking me to do.

My dad said, "I knew you were awake when your mother . . . when Zena and I were in here." He stopped for a moment. "So, you heard us talking?"

"I wasn't really listening a lot. Just for a little while. But Dad, I don't want to see her."

He nodded like he understood. Like he wasn't going to force me to do anything I didn't want to. But it must've been some kind of cop trick, because then he said, "It doesn't make sense to put this off, Aaliyah. You're going to have to see her sometime."

"Why?" I whined, sounding just like Diamond again.

"Because she's not going to go away . . . and she's your mother."

"She hasn't been."

I don't know why, but the way my dad kinda cringed made me think that I had hurt him. But that's not what I was trying to do. I wasn't mad at him—I just didn't want to see Zena.

He said, "She's always been your mother, Aaliyah. Even though she wasn't here, she gave birth to you." He took a deep breath and added, "When you were little, she used to call and ask if she could fly in to see you. But I wouldn't let her—I only wanted her to come back if she was going to stay."

Shocker! Zena had wanted to see me? I'd thought that when she'd left, she'd never thought about me again. But there had been times when she'd wanted to come back? To see me?

But I shook my head; I wasn't going to fall for that. It didn't matter if she *wanted* to come back. All that mattered was that she hadn't. She had acted as if she was *really* dead.

My dad kept on, "I was trying to protect you, sweetheart— that was always my only concern. But maybe I didn't do it the right way. Maybe I should have let her come back, even if it was just for a couple of hours or a couple of days . . . or whatever."

"No, Daddy." The thoughts about what he'd just said were moving all around in my head. But that didn't stop me from knowing that whatever had happened wasn't my dad's fault. He was the world's best dad—trust that. And I didn't want him to feel bad about anything, 'cause everything was Zena's fault.

"It's true, sweetheart," he said. "Your mother and I both played a role in what's happened. But maybe we can make things right now. Maybe we can make up for some of the time that we missed."

I couldn't remember ever hearing my father sound so sad. I wasn't sure if he felt sorry for me or himself . . . or for Zena.

He squeezed my hand. "Talk to her, just for a little while," he said. When I didn't say anything, he added, "Maybe you can do it for me."

Okay, now see—that was a straight-up dirty trick, because my dad knew that I would do anything for him, just like I knew that he would do anything for me.

And then he made it all the way bad when he added, "Please."

There was no way I could say no now, and I nodded, because I couldn't say yes out loud.

He kissed my forehead. "I'll be right back."

I waited until he walked out of the room, but the moment the door closed, I hit the floor. There wasn't a mirror in the whole doggone room—what kind of hospital was this? Then I turned to the window. Since it was dark outside, I could see my reflection. Good thing I was wearing braids—at least my hair wasn't tore up. My braids were tight. The only thing, though—I wish I had some lip gloss or something to make my face look more . . . glamorous. With the tips of my fingers, I patted my face—hard. Diamond said that got your blood flowing and gave your face a glow. When I first saw Diamond doing this, I thought my girl had lost it. But right about now, I was hoping that she was onto something. I licked my lips before I hopped back into bed.

It was a good thing that the doctor wasn't coming to check me now, because he would never let me break out of this place. Not with the way my heart was thumping. It felt like it was going to burst right out of my chest.

But even though I felt like I was going to faint again, all I did was lean back against the pillows and wait for Zena.

Chapter 5

It was really hard to look Zena straight in her face.

I don't know why, but from the moment she walked into my room, all I could do was look down at my hands.

Zena was at the side of my bed, right where India had been standing.

"How are you feeling?" she asked me.

"Fine."

"I'm sorry if . . . I didn't mean . . . I shouldn't have surprised you that way."

I shrugged and kept my eyes down. "It's okay." I don't know why I couldn't look at her. I mean, it wasn't that she wasn't beautiful. Every time I did peek up, I could see just how gorgeous she was. She looked even better than she did in her pictures in magazines.

"You have grown up to be an absolutely gorgeous young lady."

Now I couldn't help it—I had to look at her. She had just said what I had been thinking about her. I don't know why, but that saying "Like mother, like daughter" popped into my head. And I made it pop right back out.

I wasn't anything like her, 'cause there was no way I would ever leave my daughter—if I ever had one.

She said, "Your father told me that you're very smart, you're doing so well in school."

I didn't say anything, but that didn't stop her.

"I'm really proud of you."

That made me look right at her again. "You're proud of me?"

When I said that, her eyebrows rose so high, like she was surprised I was saying more than two words to her.

I asked, "Why? You didn't have anything to do with how I grew up."

Her eyebrows dropped, and so did her smile. She was hurt—not that I cared. But when I looked at my father, I did care about him. He was frowning—like he didn't like what I'd just said.

Okay, I didn't want Zena to think that I didn't have any home training. I wanted her to know that my dad had raised me right. He was big on respect, so I said, "I'm sorry."

She shook her head. "No need to be sorry. . . ." She stopped, but I could tell that there was more she wanted to say. She glanced up at my father, then back at me. "I understand how you feel." A long breath and then, "I don't want to tire you out, so I'll see you when we get to Los Angeles."

This time, it was my eyebrows that stretched to the top of my head. Was she still going to Los Angeles? Why?

I mean, it was a free country; she could go anywhere she wanted. But didn't my dad tell her that I didn't want to see her? And didn't she notice that I'd fainted because of her? And couldn't she tell that I didn't want to have anything to do with her?

I didn't care how much respect my father had taught me. Zena needed to know what was up.

"You don't have to come to Los Angeles," I said, shaking my head and looking straight in her eyes. "This was enough."

"But—"

"You can go back to Europe," I said, thinking it was a good idea to tell her exactly where to go.

Zena looked over at my father, but she didn't need to do that. There was nothing he could do. He had asked me to talk to her just one time. I'd done my part. Now it was time for her to go—for real.

After a few seconds, my father walked over and took Zena's arm. "Let me walk you outside," he said to her without looking at me.

Zena looked like she was confused or something, but she moved with him. She looked over her shoulder at me, and I stared right back. She needed to know that I wasn't playin'. Without saying good-bye, she walked out of the room with my dad.

The door closed and I let out a lot of air, 'cause I had been holding my breath big-time. When my dad came back, I knew he'd bring a long lecture with him. "Daddy-talk" was what India and I called it. But I didn't care—I would just sit and take it. 'Cause no matter what, I wasn't seeing Zena anymore. She really just needed to get on a plane and troll right back to where she came from.

I leaned back against the pillows. All of my life, I had wondered what it was going to be like to see Zena. I used to try to dream about it, but I would always stop myself because I didn't want to have even a little bit of hope. There was no need to think about something that was never going to happen.

But it did happen—she was here now. Maybe it was just for a few minutes, but she had come back.

The thing was—she hadn't come back for *me*. She'd only come back to mentor the Divine Divas, and she'd probably done that because it would help her career. I wasn't stupid enough to believe that she'd loved me before; I knew she didn't love me now.

I pulled the sheet over me, turned on my side, and closed my eyes. I hoped that my dad would come back soon. Even if he was mad at me, I couldn't wait to see him. Because if I had to lie there by myself for too long, I just knew that I was going to cry.

Chapter 6

"Thanks, Daddy," I said as my father rolled my suitcase into my bedroom.

He nodded, but that's all he did. Then he just turned away. Like he didn't want to talk to me.

It had been almost twenty-four hours since we'd seen Zena, since the doctor had released me, since we'd gone back to the hotel, gone to sleep, and then gotten up this morning to catch the ten o'clock flight back to Los Angeles. And the whole time, my father hadn't said a word about Zena.

I knew for sure that she was on his mind, 'cause he'd been real quiet. Not mad-quiet, thinking-quiet. Like Zena showing up made his head heavy. Like Zena showing up made him just as sad as it made me.

But even though I wondered what he was thinking, there was no way I was going to bring up Zena. I mean, it was bad enough that I couldn't stop thinking about her. I didn't want to talk about her, too.

My father turned around, kissed me on my forehead, and

25

said, "Why don't you lie down for a little while? I'll whip up something for us to eat."

I nodded, even though I wasn't tired or hungry and when my dad closed the door, I plopped down on my bed and let out a long, long breath of air.

It was hard to believe that so much had happened in my life. Last time I had lain down on this bed, life was breezy. But this had been some kind of trip—full of ups and downs. First, there was the big up of even being in New York and staying in that fab suite at that tight hotel. That first night was like whoa—I had so much fun just hanging with my girls and Arjay and Troy and Riley. Then there was the big down when Veronique went missing. I mean, could things get any scarier than that? When Diamond told us that Veronique had left the hotel and might have been kidnapped, I was straight-up scared. But then Arjay did that Superman thing and rescued my girl. And then we were way, way up after we sang and won. Nothing in the world was better than that.

But then Zena showed up and took the whole trip way down. Why did she have to come back so that now everyone would know that I'd been lying? Why did she have to come back so that now everyone would know that she never wanted to be my mother?

I jumped up from my bed, but before I went to my closet, I checked the door to make sure it was closed all the way. Then I pulled down the huge treasure chest that my father had given to me when I was five years old. Sitting back on my bed, I stared at the golden box. I bet my dad didn't even know that I still had this.

But forget about the box—all I could think about was Zena.

There had been so many days when I'd dreamed about her coming back. It wasn't like my dreams had a lot of stuff in them, because I couldn't even remember Zena. The only pictures that were in my head were from the stories that my dad used to tell me about her. When I was really little, I wasn't even mad that she was gone—I just thought that everybody's mother went away.

Until I was in the first grade. That's when I saw Diamond's and India's moms and how they were always in church and on class trips and at our ballet recitals. That's when I asked my dad when my mom would be coming back. And that's when he started giving me that story line: "Oh, baby, your mother really loved you, but she had to go away. She can't come back."

For a long time, I couldn't figure it out. Not until that day I was seven years old and looking at the cover of *Ebony* magazine. My dad came over and sat next to me on the couch. That's when he told me that the pretty lady in the picture was my mother.

At first, I didn't believe him. I mean, that lady in the magazine didn't look anything like the lady in the pictures that my dad had around the house.

After that, anytime my father tried to tell me that Zena really loved me, all I did was say, "Yeah, right." Well, I only said that on the inside, not on the outside. No way was I going to let my dad hear me say that. But whenever he talked about Zena, it just sounded like blah, blah, blah to me.

I didn't cry in front of my dad, but I cried a lot when I went to bed. My mother was Zena! It didn't take a nuclear physicist to figure it out—she left because she didn't love me. She didn't want to be my mother; she wanted to be Zena.

That's when I started telling people that my mother was dead. It was easy, because my dad just never talked about it and he never heard me tell that lie. I didn't have to say it a lot—once you told people that your mother was dead, they felt sorry for you and just left you alone.

But even though I tried to believe that Zena was dead, it was hard to pretend, when Zena was all over the place. The more I tried to get rid of her in my mind, the more I saw her on TV or heard her on the radio. No matter what I did, she was always in front of my face.

"Sweetheart."

I almost jumped off the bed when I heard my father. I grabbed my treasure box and kicked it under the bed before I yelled out, "Yes?"

My dad opened the door. "I ordered a pizza." He smiled a little. "Even added pineapples."

Okay, he was definitely trying to make me feel better, because my dad hated pineapples on pizza.

Just when he was about to close the door, I yelled out, "Daddy, why did Zena have to come back?"

I didn't really mean to ask him that, but I guess all the thoughts in my head just kinda came out. My father looked at me for a moment before he let out a big ole sigh.

That made me really sorry that I had said anything. "If you don't want to talk about it . . ."

He shook his head and sat on the edge of my bed. "No, this is good. We have to talk; I was just waiting until you were ready."

I sat down next to him and he took my hand. "Your mother may not have done it right, but she came back because of you. She wants to be a part of your life. And now that she's here—"

I didn't even let him finish. "I don't want her to stay."

My dad stayed quiet for a second. "She's going to stay, sweetheart." He said it as if that was a fact. "So we have to decide what to do."

Decide? What was there to decide? "I don't want to have anything to do with her."

"Aaliyah, you can't talk that way about your mother."

"Why not? That's how she talked about me."

He frowned. "She never said that about you."

"How do you know? Oh, that's right," I said and jumped up from the bed. "She probably never said *anything* about me. She never told anybody she had a daughter. She never even said that she was married."

Okay, for the second day in a row, I could tell that I had hurt my father's feelings. That's not what I wanted to do, but I had to tell it!

"What your mother did was not right, sweetheart. I know that. And it hurts me that you're hurt."

"It's not your fault, Daddy."

But he kept on talking, like he hadn't heard me. "The thing is, none of that matters if we can fix it now. If she wants to come back, that can only be a good thing."

I didn't get my dad. Why was he being so understanding? Zena hadn't left just me—she had left him, too. "How can you say that? How can you just forgive her?"

"The truth is, I forgave your mother a long time ago. How could I stay angry with her? She gave me the greatest gift— you."

"But she *left* us. She just threw us away."

"No," my dad said, shaking his head. "Don't you ever say that. That's not the way it was." He sighed, like talking about this made him really tired. "I don't know how to explain it all to you, but she didn't throw you away."

"That's the way it feels to me."

"I know. But to tell you the truth, I'm not sure how good she would have been if she'd stayed, Aaliyah. She had this dream and—"

I didn't even let him finish that tired old story he'd told me before. "All I know is that mothers just don't give away their children."

He nodded slowly. The look in his eyes told me that he understood me but didn't agree. "This situation is complicated. It's going to take you a while to understand it."

"Why do I have to understand anything?" I poked my lips out so that he would know how really mad I was. I felt like a brat, but I couldn't help it. I wanted him to be on my side.

"The fact is, Aaliyah, your mother is here. She arrived this morning and she's not going away."

"She's in L.A.?" I moaned. I felt like I was going to be sick. "I told her that I didn't want her to come here," I said like I really thought she would listen to me.

"She's here and I'm glad."

Traitor! was what I wanted to scream, but I wasn't crazy. So all I did was cross my arms and try to stare him down. This time, I *wanted* my dad to feel bad.

But it was like he didn't care how I was acting. "You're growing up. You need your mother now."

Okay, my dad was really losing it.

"Now you two will be able to get to know one another."

I decided not to say another thing, because my father just wasn't hearing me.

When I stayed quiet, he said, "You're going to have to find a way to handle this, sweetheart, because she's going to be your mentor."

"Nuh-uh." I was shaking my head so hard, I knew I would have a headache in a minute. "I don't want her to be the Divine Divas mentor."

"Sweetheart," my dad began, moving his hands in the air, "we can't go to the record company and tell them that you don't want to work with Zena."

"Why not?"

"Because Mr. Hamilton already explained that you girls are being tested. Remember what he said—sometimes you're going to have to do things you don't want to do. Sometimes you're going to have to sing when you don't want to sing. They're training you girls to be professionals."

"Then Zena needs to quit."

"She's not going to do that."

"You can make her quit, Daddy."

"I'm not going to do that."

Why not? My dad could do anything that he really wanted to do.

"Well then, if she doesn't quit"—I bit my lip for a second—"then I will."

That was a shocker! I couldn't believe I'd said that. And the way my dad stared at me, he couldn't believe it either.

"Aaliyah." He said my name so softly, so sadly. "This is not the mature way to handle this."

It was the disappointment I heard in his voice that made the tears come to my eyes. But I wasn't backing down. "If she's the mentor, then I'm dropping out of the Divine Divas."

Now my dad looked beyond disappointed; he looked upset. He looked so sad that I almost changed my mind. I never wanted to do anything to disappoint him, never wanted to take the chance that he might leave me, too.

But I kept my lips pressed together. I couldn't take back what I'd said because it was what I really felt.

My father stared at me for a couple more seconds before he said, "You have to do what you have to do." Then he turned away and didn't look at me as he walked to the door. "I'll let you know when the pizza gets here."

The moment he stepped out of my room, the tears rolled down my face. I just hoped that my dad wasn't really, really mad at me. I mean, how could he not understand?

I tried to do the Big S—suck it up—but the tears kept right on coming. Lying back down on my bed, I thought about how in September when Diamond first told us about this contest, I didn't really want to be part of the group. I was just doing it to be with my girls. But then we started winning, and now we were just one more win away from the big time. I wanted to be right there—in South Beach—with my best friends, standing on the stage when we shut the whole contest down.

But none of that was going to happen. Not if Zena stayed.

I sunk my head into my pillow. It was a good thing that I had other dreams: Harvard, being a nuclear physicist. Because the dream of being a winner with my girls was now so over!

Chapter 7

Even though I wanted to, I couldn't put this off any longer. I had to talk to my girls.

"I cannot wait for school to be over." Diamond slammed her locker.

"What are you talking about?" Veronique asked. "School is over."

"For *today*," Diamond, said as if being here was so hard. "But we have to come back tomorrow and then again on Monday and the next day and the next day and—"

Veronique held up her hand. "I get it."

"I don't understand why we have to do this," Diamond whined. "What's the purpose of sitting through math and French and chemistry when we're not going to need any of this when we're stars?"

"Well before we become stars," Veronique came back, "we have to get through finals. Sybil said we're not going to start serious rehearsals until after our tests."

"See—that's what I'm talking about. This stuff is getting

in our way," Diamond pointed out. "We don't have as much time to practice as before. July fourth is only six weeks away, and what we need to be doing is setting it up so we can shut it down in Miami."

"So, what are you sayin'?" Veronique asked.

"I'm sayin' that we're celebrities and celebrities don't have to go to school. Celebrities have more important things to do."

India and Veronique looked at me as if they were waiting for me to jump all over Diamond, because that was just how we rolled—she would say something dumb, then I would straighten her out. But I had too much on my mind to get into it with Diamond right now.

So when I stayed quiet, India said, "Everybody has to go to school, Diamond. Even celebrities."

She rolled her eyes as if India didn't know what she was talking about. "Do you think Beyoncé went to school? Or Ciara? Or Rihanna?"

"They *all* went to school," Veronique piped in.

"I don't know why. They're like ga-millionaires now. Who needs school when you have that much money?"

"First of all," Veronique said, "we don't have the money."

"It's coming."

"And if we win the contest"—this time it was India who spoke—"we're not going to get that much."

"Duh, that's because it's our first contract. But once our first single hits the charts," she raised her hand and snapped her fingers in the air with every word, "it . . . will . . . be . . . all . . . over."

India shook her head. "I don't care if we're going to make ten ga-million, do you think our parents are going to let us drop out of school?"

Veronique added, "And don't even talk about Pastor Ford. She'll beat our butts up and down this hallway if we even think about dropping out."

Diamond rolled her eyes, and then, for the first time, she looked at me. "Well, what do you have to say, Miss I-Love-School-More-Than-Anything?"

I shrugged. "India's right. Our parents will never go for it."

Diamond frowned. "That's it? You don't have anything else? What about something like"—and then she made her voice higher to sound like mine—"Diamond, what's wrong with you? Everybody loves school! Only a fool would want to drop out." She stopped and waited for me to say something. When I didn't, she put her hand on my shoulder. "Okay, what's up? 'Cause if you're not on my case, something's wrong."

"Leave Aaliyah alone," India insisted. "She just got out of the hospital."

I said, "I'm fine," like I'd been telling them all day. This was my first day back, because my dad had made me stay home yesterday, too, just to be sure that I was feeling better. But I was so glad to be back here. At home, all I did was think about Zena, but here, there was so much going on that she hardly came in my mind.

"So, why are you so quiet?" Diamond demanded.

I shrugged.

She grinned. "I bet I know. You got to hang out with your mom all day yesterday, didn't you?" Before I could even tell Diamond not to call Zena my mom, she leaned against the lockers and said, "How cool is this? I'm best friends with Zena's daughter."

On any other day, I would've been mad at Diamond for finding a way to make this all about her. But truth—I had used up all of my mad being mad at Zena.

"I need to tell you guys something," I said, finally ready to face them.

That made Diamond stand up straight. "So you *did* hang with her! I knew it. Why didn't you hit me up? I would've zoomed right over there." She stomped her foot like she was one of Veronique's little brothers.

"You're going to have plenty of time to hang with Zena." Veronique waved her hand like Zena was no big deal. "Since she's going to be our mentor."

"That's what I want to talk to you guys about." I took a deep breath. "I need a solid."

Veronique shrugged. "Ride or die. We do whatever for each other."

I nodded. That made me feel a little better; like Veronique always said, we were more than friends, we were sisters.

Right after I took a deep breath, I said, "We have to find a way to get Zena out." All of their eyes got big, but I kept on. "Because if we don't, then I'm quitting the group."

"What!" all three of them said at the same time. And the way they sounded, you could tell that we'd been singing together. They each hit their note perfectly.

"You can't quit," Diamond said as if she could tell me what to do.

"I don't want to; that's why I need your help to get Zena out."

"I want Zena to be our mentor!" Diamond shouted as if she was the only one who counted. "Do you know who she is?"

I gave Diamond the look—the one that let her know that I thought that was not the smartest question.

Veronique put up her hand. "Hold up," she said, stopping Diamond from continuing her attack. Then, to me she asked, "You don't wanna work with your mom?"

"I wish you all would stop calling her that." The way Veronique looked at me made me sorry that I had snapped that way. But dang, didn't they get it? She wasn't a mother to me. Calming down a little bit, I said, "No, I don't want to work with her. And if I have to, then I'm quitting."

"You can't do that!" Diamond yelled, even though we were standing in the middle of the hallway. But none of the other kids even looked at us. Everybody had their own end-of-the-school-day drama going on. "If you quit, then it's over for all of us. Remember, we have to finish like we started."

My heart was beating fast now, because I'd been afraid that one of my girls would bring that up. It's not like I wanted to ruin it for Diamond, India, or Veronique, but what was I supposed to do? This was the deal: As long as Zena was in, I was out.

But even though my heart was pounding, I shrugged like it was no biggie. "They made an exception for India in the San Francisco contest. They can make another one and let me drop out."

"They made the exception for India because it was real—she was sick. But this . . . this is stupid. What're we going to say? One of the singers is quitting because she doesn't want to work with the biggest star in the world, who happens to be her mother?"

I slammed my locker door so hard, it made everything around us shake. Especially my girls—they were shaking like I had scared them for real. And I was glad, because now I *was* mad. There was no way Diamond should've called me stupid.

My books fell to the floor, my fingers curled into fists, and Diamond's eyes got wide—like she thought I might really try to beat her up.

"Take that back," I said, even though now I sounded stupid to myself.

"Take back what?" Her eyes got even bigger, like she was really scared. But I had to give her props, because she wasn't backing down, even though we both knew that I could take her—just like I'd done in the second grade.

"You called me stupid," I growled.

"No, I didn't." It didn't look like she was scared anymore. Now she just looked mad. As mad as I was. She stepped so close to me that there was nothing but a little bit of air between us. "What I *said* was that the *idea* of you quitting was stupid. Not you."

"It's the same thing," I yelled.

Veronique jumped in between us and pushed Diamond back. Then India pushed me back, too.

"You guys stop it," Veronique demanded like she was one of our parents. "It's not supposed to go down like this with us. We're sistahs, remember?"

"She's not my sister if she plans on ruining my life!" Diamond yelled, then she turned around and stomped away, her ponytail swishing on her head like the tail on a horse.

I let out a deep breath, not believing that I had gone there. I always got mad at Diamond for something, but I hadn't jumped in her face like that since we were seven years old.

"Are you okay?" India asked in a voice that sounded like she felt sorry for me.

"Yeah." I picked up my books.

"Wow. For a minute," Veronique said, helping me with my bag, "I thought you and Diamond were really going to go at it."

That made me feel bad, because I was supposed to be the mature one. But this thing with Zena didn't make me feel mature at all.

"Do you really want to drop out?" India asked.

Okay, this was just getting worse, because all I had to do was look at India and Veronique and see that even though they were going to be on my side—ride or die—the Divine Divas was big for them, too.

I was getting tired of crying, but I could still feel the tears coming to my eyes. *Please, God. Don't let me be a big ole baby right here in front of everybody.*

Before the first tear could roll down my face, my BFFL took my hand and dragged me down the hall and out of the school before I made a fool of myself. Veronique followed us, and we didn't stop until we were on the side of the school where no one could see us.

Before she said anything, India hugged me. "We'll figure this out."

"Yeah," Veronique added when she gave me a hug, too. "We can talk to Pastor Ford. Pastor can fix anything."

I nodded, because I couldn't speak. Thank God for my friends—at least India and Veronique. I knew they didn't understand, but they didn't need to. All they cared about was me.

"Okay," I sniffed, hoping I could keep back the rest of my tears.

Then without saying anything else, the three of us walked toward the bus stop. The same way we did every day. As if everything was normal.

But what was normal before was nowhere near normal now.

Chapter 8

"Aaliyah!" my dad called out. "The phone's for you."

"Thanks, Dad." I pushed myself off the bed even though it wasn't even eight o'clock. But I was really tired. Not body-tired, just mind-tired.

I grabbed the extension in the hallway, wondering who was calling me at home rather than on my cell. But the moment I said, "Hello," I knew what was up.

"She's on now, Pastor," my father said. "Thanks so much."

"I'll speak to you later, Heber." And then, when she heard the click, Pastor Ford said to me, "How're you feeling, Aaliyah?"

I leaned against the wall, then scooted down until I was sitting on the carpet. "I'm fine."

"I wanted to come by and see you, but I was called out of town. I'm in Alabama right now."

Dang! The news had traveled all the way to the other side of the country? I couldn't believe my dad had tracked Pastor down like that. But then in the next second, Pastor told me the real deal.

"Diamond called me."

Oh, brother. I should have known. Diamond—straight-up drama.

"So," Pastor Ford began, "do you want to tell me what's going on?"

I tried to imagine exactly what Diamond had said. Knowing her, she had probably called Pastor screaming and crying and telling her that I was destroying the whole world. "Didn't Diamond tell you?" I asked, not really wanting to get into this with my pastor right now.

"Well, I called to talk to *you*," Pastor said straight up. Like she didn't care if I had an attitude. "So, tell me what's going on."

What was I supposed to say? Diamond was the one who had said it, but I was sure that everybody thought I was being stupid. Even my dad was still talking to me about doing the mature thing.

"Aaliyah?"

"Yes." I took a deep breath. Since she wanted to hear it, I was going to tell it. "I don't want to be in the group anymore if Zena is going to be our mentor because I don't want to work with her," I said real fast. "I don't want her to come back here now, because she never wanted to be my mother before. So why does she want to be here now?" I closed my eyes and waited for Pastor to tell me that she thought I was stupid, too.

"I understand," Pastor Ford said softly.

My eyes popped wide open. Nobody had said that—nobody had told me that they understood. Not even India.

She said, "I cannot imagine how hard this is for you, sweetheart. And I wish I'd known before this all happened. Glory 2 God came to me and Sybil, and we were excited that you girls were going to work with Zena."

"So you didn't know she was my . . ." I couldn't even make myself say it.

But Pastor knew what I was talking about, and she answered me anyway. "No, I didn't."

Shocker! I thought Pastor Ford knew just about everything.

She said, "But you girls have worked too hard to stop the Divine Divas now."

"I don't want to stop," I said. "I just don't want to be part of it." I was so tired of saying the same thing over and over.

"The thing is, Aaliyah, the record company has contracted these singers to work with the groups. Unless there's something major—"

"This is major, Pastor. Why can't they just switch mentors? We can work with someone else."

Pastor Ford sighed. "I think the other groups have already started working with their mentors, and they did come to us first. . . ." When she stopped this time, I thought I heard something like a pencil tapping on a table. "Let me talk to Roberto. I'll see what I can do."

For the first time since I had looked into Zena's face the other day, I had some hope. "Thank you."

"Okay, we'll talk; I'll see you Sunday."

After I clicked off the phone, I just sat there, staring at the floor. I didn't want to be such a drama queen, but what else was I supposed to do?

That was when I felt them, the tears coming back—again!

"Dang!" I tried to wipe the tears away, but they kept coming. I pushed myself from the floor, slammed down the phone, turned around, and bumped right into my father.

I don't know why, but the first thing that came to my mind was, "I'm sorry, Daddy."

All he said was, "I know, sweetheart." And then he hugged me and held me until I couldn't cry anymore.

Chapter 9

I couldn't sleep.

The thoughts just stayed in my head. Thoughts of Zena and the Divine Divas. Thoughts of how I was ruining everything for everybody.

When I rolled over and looked at the clock, I couldn't believe it. It wasn't even midnight, but I felt like I had been turning over and over for hours.

I pushed myself up from the bed and looked around. What was I supposed to do? And then I remembered something— my dad used to give me warm milk when I was a little girl and couldn't sleep. Maybe that would help me now.

After I tied my bathrobe around me, I tiptoed to the door and opened it slowly so that it wouldn't creak and wake up my dad.

But when I walked to the top of the stairs, I stopped. The light was on downstairs, and by the time I tiptoed down two steps, I heard him talking.

"Zena, just listen to me."

My heart started beating fast; was Zena downstairs? Was she in my house? But when I didn't hear anything else, I realized that he was talking on the phone. Good thing, because I might have had a heart attack if she ever came to our house.

Slowly, I sat down on the step and listened.

"Is there anything you can do?" my father asked.

I wished I could hear what she was saying, but when my father sighed, I knew she wasn't saying anything I wanted to hear.

My dad said, "You don't have to explain contracts to me. But I also know that contracts can be broken." Then, he was quiet again before he said, "I'm not trying to keep you away from her," his voice a little bit higher now. "I've talked to her, but she won't budge." More quiet and then, "Well, Zena, what did you expect?"

There was no need for me to hear any more, and I got up and went back into my bedroom. I don't even know why I took off my bathrobe and got back into bed—there was no way I was going to be able to sleep now.

This was some straight-up mess for sure. I wasn't backing down, and it seemed like Zena wasn't going to either. Would she really stay and push me out of the group? Maybe that was her plan all along. Maybe she really did hate me.

It was hard to believe that this was happening. My life was about to be ruined, and it was all Zena's fault.

Chapter 10

Diamond was seriously hatin'.

She hadn't said a single word to me. Not in school on Friday, and she hadn't even called yesterday, begging for me to go to some mall with her like she did every Saturday. She was acting like I was invisible.

Like right now, here we were in church, sitting in our regular seats, and Diamond was acting like I had never been born.

"Do you have an extra pen?" Diamond turned around and whispered to India even though she had to reach over me.

Both of us knew that Diamond didn't need a pen. There were three things Diamond always had inside one of the designer bags she always carried: lip gloss, one of her parents' credit cards, and a pen—just in case someone recognized her and wanted her autograph. But she had made the point to talk straight to India—in the middle of the sermon—just to continue the hate.

Well, I didn't care. Diamond could keep the drama going, and while she did that, I was going to keep doing me.

Not that I didn't feel bad, and not that I wasn't scared. I knew that whatever I decided to do could shut down the whole thing for my girls. But I just felt that there had to be a way for me to win. I mean, it didn't take a nuclear physicist to figure this out. All the grown-ups—my dad, Pastor Ford, Sybil—had to do was find a way for the Divine Divas to get a new mentor. What was so hard about that?

India poked me in my arm. "Stand up," she whispered.

I was so deep in my head that I hadn't even noticed that Pastor had started the benediction. When I stood up, my heart started beating fast, just like it did the other day . . . and I hoped that I wasn't going to faint again. After I took a deep breath, I calmed down a little, but I was still scared.

It was getting closer to the time when I would have to speak to Pastor. She called this morning and told my dad that she wanted to talk to me—alone—after the second service. It was the alone part that had me worried.

After we all said, "Amen," and Pastor told everyone to have a blessed week, I swung my purse over my arm and said to India, "I'll see you later; I'm going to see Pastor."

India nodded and hugged me, but all of a sudden, Diamond was all up in my face.

"Pastor? You're going to see Pastor?"

I raised my eyebrows, crossed my arms, and answered her by not saying anything at all.

Diamond folded her arms, too, and gave me one of those sistah-girl head twists. "All I want to know is if you're going to see Pastor about us." She poked her finger in her chest, then pointed to India and Veronique. "Are you going to talk about the Divine Divas?" she asked, as if I wasn't part of the group.

I rolled my eyes, looked at India, and said, "I'll call you later." I didn't say anything to Diamond or Veronique. Not that I was dissing my girl Vee, but she was standing so close to Diamond, I couldn't say anything to her.

I was sure my girls were watching me as I went down from the balcony, then through the sanctuary. But by the time I got to the hall that led to Pastor's office, I wasn't thinking anything about India, Veronique, or Diamond. All that was on my mind was that I wished I could go home and forget about this meeting. Not that going home would do anything, 'cause if I didn't show up, Pastor would be at my front door in a minute, dragging me right back here.

I wasn't about to diss Pastor. She was one of the three grown-ups I never messed with: God, my dad, and Pastor Ford.

"Hey, Aaliyah!" Etta-Marie, Pastor Ford's assistant, greeted me as if I was walking into a party or something. The way she was grinning made my hope go all the way up. If Etta-Marie was all happy like this, maybe Pastor Ford had some good news for me. I knew it—I knew Pastor would have my back!

"Pastor's waiting for you," Etta-Marie pointed to the door. "Just go right on in."

I took a deep breath even though I didn't feel so scared anymore. Not that I was afraid of Pastor. No way; she had been so great to me. The truth—she felt like a mother, and since I was a little girl, I knew I could talk to her about anything . . . well, almost everything; I had never said a word to her about Zena.

So it wasn't my pastor that still had my heart beating kind of hard. It was just not knowing what she was going to say.

Pastor was standing up behind her desk, as if she was waiting for me. "Hi, sweetheart."

The way she was smiling, too, just like Etta-Marie, made me kind of happy. This was going to be good news; I was going to be able to stay with my girls. We were still the Divine Divas, and the way I saw it, we were going to win this contest.

She came from around her desk and hugged me tight. Now I was even happier. Just by the way she held me, I knew that everything was going to be all right.

"Let's sit down here." She pointed to the couch. "I'm going to have some coffee; do you want some juice?"

I nodded and watched as she poured me a glass from one of the fancy bottles that she had on a long table against the wall. Whenever I came into Pastor's office, the table was covered with food. I could see a bowl of fruit and then a plate full of donuts. It almost felt like Pastor and I were about to have a party—like there was something big to celebrate.

I was even more sure of that when Pastor handed me a glass of orange juice and a glazed donut. Right when I took my first bite, Pastor sat down next to me and said, "So, I talked to Roberto Hamilton."

When she smiled, I smiled. This was why I loved my pastor so much. She felt me. I'd taken my problem to her, and she'd fixed it. She was off the freakin' chain!

I took another bite and wondered what Pastor Ford had gotten Roberto Hamilton, the president of Glory 2 God Productions, to do. Was he going to just trade Zena for another mentor who was already working with one of the other groups? Or were they going to fire her completely? I know it wasn't right—especially since I was sitting in church—but I was feelin' the firing thing.

Pastor said, "Roberto told me that the mentors can't be changed, and if we can't work with Zena, then the Divine Divas will be disqualified."

The way Pastor said that, like it was no big deal, made me first think that I hadn't heard her right. It was the big ole bite that I'd just taken out of my donut that made me not scream out. But I yelled on the inside. I wanted to know what she was talking about.

It took me a minute to swallow everything, then I looked at Pastor like she was crazy or something. "We're going to be disqualified?"

Pastor Ford shook her head. "Only if you refuse to work with Zena."

She was just talking like we were having a regular conversation. But there was nothing regular about this. My heart was back to beating hard, and I had to keep taking deep breaths.

"But that doesn't make sense. Why couldn't Mr. Roberto do something?"

When Pastor Ford raised her eyebrows, I realized that I was talking kinda loud. So I took another deep breath and lowered my voice. "I don't understand, Pastor."

She said, "You have quite a bit to learn about the music business."

The only reason I didn't roll my eyes was because, like I just said, Pastor Ford was one of those adults I never dissed. But she was starting to get on my nerves. I didn't understand the music business? As if she did! What did she know that I didn't?

And then, as if she could hear what I was thinking, she said, "In this business, just like others, when plans have been set in motion, sometimes the plans are not so easy to change. It seems like Glory 2 God has already done a lot of publicity for Zena and the Divine Divas, and they're not willing to pull back all the money they've spent without a good reason."

"But I have a good reason."

"Not to them."

"So we're going to be kicked out, just like that?"

She shook her head. "No one said a thing about kicking you out. Everyone wants the Divine Divas to be part of this competition."

Then, the way she kept quiet, I knew what she was

thinking—that I was the only one messing everything up. That was when I felt them—the tears in my eyes. Again!

Pastor Ford scooted closer to me on the sofa. "Aaliyah, sweetheart, talk to me about Zena. Talk to me about your mother."

"She's not my mother!" I said, pushing the tears from my cheek. I was so mad at myself. Why was I crying? I didn't want one more tear to come out of my eyes about Zena.

"She *is* your mother, baby. No matter what you say"— she slowed down, as if that would help me understand her better—"she's . . . your . . . mother."

I shook my head as hard as I could. "Mothers are people who are there when you need them. Mothers want to be with their children."

Pastor Ford put her arms around me and rested my head on her shoulder. "You are a wise young girl," she said softly. "But there are things that you may not understand yet."

"I understand that I wish Zena had never come back. I understand that I hate her."

"No, you don't," Pastor whispered.

"Yes, I do!" I said, sitting up straight. "She didn't love me and I hate her." Even though Pastor didn't say anything, I could tell that she didn't like what I was saying. "I know it's bad for me to hate, Pastor, and I know that God is probably mad at me, but it's Zena's fault."

Pastor Ford shook her head. "You think you hate her because you think that hate is the opposite of love. But it's not—the opposite of love is indifference. And you're a long way from indifference."

I didn't care what Pastor called it—hate, indifference—it was the same to me.

I had been so sure that Pastor was going to take care of this for me. Now what was I going to do? And what about my girls? India and Veronique. And Diamond? I couldn't even begin to think about her. We'd been best friends since the third grade, but after this, Diamond and I would never be friends again.

Pastor made me raise my head and look at her. "You don't hate your mother," she said as if I would agree with her when she said it this time. "You're just hurt, and you have every right to be. But look at it this way—this might be a good way to get to know your mother."

"Why would I want to know her when she never wanted to know me?"

Pastor sighed like now I was getting on her nerves, but she didn't sound that way when she asked, "Did you ever stop to think that maybe this is God?"

God? Why would He make me go through all of this?

She kept on, "Maybe God sent Zena back and set this all up because it was time. Maybe God wanted your mother to come back and this was the best way."

"I don't think God would do this to me."

"This is not a punishment, sweetheart. This is an opportunity."

Please! Now I wished Pastor would just stop talking. How was this an opportunity? There was *nothing* good about this.

"There is one thing I know," Pastor said as she stood up and walked to her desk. When she came back to me, I knew I was in trouble, because she was holding her Bible. "I know that God didn't bring you and the other girls along in this competition for you to drop out now." She opened the Bible, then passed it to me. "Read this," she said, pointing out a scripture in Proverbs.

The last thing I wanted to do was read something from the Bible. But there was no way I was going to say no to pastor *and* to God. Being mad didn't make me crazy.

" 'An unfriendly man pursues selfish ends; he defies all sound judgment. A fool finds no pleasure in understanding but delights in airing his own opinion.' "

"Do you know what that means?"

I was thinking it meant that Pastor thought I was a selfish fool, but I just shook my head.

She said, "Sometimes we get so mad and caught up in our own thoughts and opinions that we can't even hear anyone else; we can't listen to reason." And as if that wasn't enough, she had to really go and beat me down. "There're lots of reasons for you to be upset with this situation, and I empathize with you. But there aren't any reasons for you to selfishly take this dream away from everyone else. You really don't have a good reason to drop out. There're so many people depending on you, including God."

That's not fair! I always heard grown-ups talking about the race card, but Pastor was playing the God card, and there was nothing as bad as that.

"So, am I supposed to just do it so that everybody else will be happy? What about me?"

"God will take care of you. He'll give you everything you need to keep going. He'll give you the strength, He'll give you the wisdom—whatever it is you need in order to work with your mother and get to know her better."

I didn't say anything out loud, but inside, I was shaking my head.

Pastor Ford took my hand, then looked me in my eyes. "Here's the thing, Aaliyah. I can tell you what I think, but only you can do what's in your heart. The final decision is yours. If you can't find a way to work with your mother, I'm sure everyone will understand." Before I could say anything, she stood up. "I need to check on something with Etta-Marie." That was all she said, and then she was gone.

Even after I was by myself for a couple of minutes, I still didn't move. I wanted to get up, leave this office, and go tell everybody that the Divine Divas were so over.

Then I looked around, and I knew why Pastor had left me by myself. She had left me with all these Bibles and other books—all about God. She had left me here surrounded by Him.

But that didn't change anything for me. Pastor was always saying that God knew our heart. Well then, He would understand why I had to do what I had to do.

It was in my heart to drop out, but my head was saying something else. How *could* I do this to my friends? And even though Diamond got on all of my nerves, all of the time, this was her dream, and she had taken me, India, and Veronique—her crew—with her. Because she loved us.

My head was down when I heard Pastor's door open, and it wasn't until he sat down next to me that I saw that it wasn't Pastor, but my dad who had come in. And just like Pastor Ford did a little while ago, my dad hugged me.

He didn't say anything while the tears slowly ran down my cheeks. But I didn't cry for long. There was nothing left to cry about. The grown-ups had made their decision, and I had made mine. It was time for me to just stand up and do what I had to do.

I just prayed that I would be able to live with the consequences.

Chapter 11

My father rolled the car to a stop right in front of the church. For the first time ever in life, I didn't want to go inside. All I wanted my father to do was take me home.

But like everyone always said—I was the mature one. So I just needed to handle it.

I put my hand on the car door, but that was it. My legs wouldn't move. All I could do was stare at the building, with the bright, colorful windows and the golden steeple on top.

"Do you want me to go in there with you?" my dad asked so softly that I almost didn't hear him.

Before I turned to face him, I put a smile on my face. Like I was brave and I was cool. "I'm okay," I said as if that were the truth.

Even though I was a little scared, I meant what I said. Once I had made up my mind last Sunday in Pastor Ford's office to do this, I was gonna do it all the way. That's just how I rolled. I'd made the decision to keep the Divine Divas together, and we were going to win this competition—with

Zena. Then, after that, she could just step right back out of my life.

My dad smiled back at me, then squeezed my hand like he was trying to give me some courage. "You know, I still think it would have been better if we'd met with your mother first."

Inside I sighed—I never would have made that sound out loud—but I sure hated it when he called Zena my mother. I hated when anybody called her that.

But that wasn't the only thing. Since last week, everybody had been telling me the same thing . . . that I needed to meet with Zena before this rehearsal. But why would I do that? She wasn't any more special to me than some lady on the street. Just like Diamond, India, and Veronique, I was going to meet Zena tonight—and that was it.

Even though I was mad that he had called Zena my mother, I kept the smile on my face because I didn't want my dad to worry about me. "I'm going to be all right," I said, then I kissed him on the cheek and jumped out of the car.

Before I could close the door, he told me that he'd be right here to pick me up. I kinda laughed, because my father hardly ever came to meet me anymore. Since Diamond had gotten her car, I always rode with her. But I knew what was up; he was going to be sitting right here in the car—probably early—to make sure that I came out of this alive. Well, he didn't need to worry about me. Now, Zena? That was another story.

I waved and then turned toward the church as if I wasn't afraid of a thing. But truth—there was a lot of big talk coming out of my mouth. Inside I really was afraid.

Right when I got to the door, I shook my head trying to shake away all my bad thoughts. It was gonna be all right—all I had to do was the big S and act like none of this really bothered me. Because truth—it didn't. I wasn't affected by Zena at all.

Handle it, Aaliyah, was what I kept saying to myself.

The moment I pulled open the door to the learning center part of the church where we practiced, India bum-rushed me and almost knocked me down.

"Why did you turn off your cell phone?" she demanded like she was the boss of me.

I shrugged; it was true—I had turned off my cell right after my last class. And I didn't meet my girls like I always did after school at our lockers because I knew they would want to talk about tonight. They would have asked me a million questions and I didn't want to deal with this until we got here.

"Are you all right?" India whispered.

I looked at my BFFL and nodded. "Yeah, why wouldn't I be?"

"Because. . . ." And she stopped, as if that was her whole answer.

"It's no big deal," I said, pushing past her. And then, to prove that I was okay, I put on a big ole smile and waved to everybody. "Hey, y'all. Hey, Diamond. Hey, Vee. Hey, Arjay." I went down the line.

But I guess I didn't really fool anybody because by the time I got to the other side of the room, my girls were all over me.

"Are you going to be all right?" Diamond demanded.

I took a deep breath before I turned to her. "Yes," I said, still smiling. "I wish everybody would stop asking me that."

"I just want to make sure that everything's going to go down the way it's supposed to."

"Don't worry, Diamond," I said, but my smile was gone. "I won't do anything to ruin this for you."

"I'm just sayin'," and then she didn't finish saying anything. She just walked away.

Veronique rolled her eyes. "You know she does love you, right?"

I laughed a little bit. "Yeah, I know."

"And you know we love you, too, right?" India added.

"That I know for sure."

"Good!" Veronique said. " 'Cause we got your back. If anything happens . . ."

"Nothing's going to happen. My dad talked to Zena and told her not to make a big deal out of tonight. She's just going to treat me like everybody else."

Veronique frowned. "You okay with that?"

"Yeah, 'cause I am just like everybody else. And she's just an ordinary singer to me."

I ignored the way India and Veronique looked at each other—like they knew something I didn't. The two of them walked away, but I was by myself for just a couple of seconds when Troy came over and slid down on the floor next to me.

"I've left you a couple of messages," he said. "Wanted to catch up with you to make sure that you were all right."

I nodded. "I'm sorry I didn't call you back. Been kinda busy."

His smile was lopsided when he said, "You know, you could give a brotha a complex not returning phone calls."

I laughed. "I'm not trying to do that." Then I got serious. "I've just . . . been going through stuff."

"Yeah." The way he stopped and looked at me, I knew what was coming next—like everybody else, he was going to ask or say something about Zena. "So, here's the deal—we should go out sometime. You know, just me and you. Away from the group. And we can talk about anything that you want to talk about." He grinned at me. "Or not."

Shocker! He didn't want to talk about Zena? I thought that was all that was on everybody's mind. Even though India and Veronique were trying to play this like it was all cool, I knew they wanted me to talk about her, too.

But Troy didn't seem to care about anything except for me. And that's why I said, "I'll give you a call over the weekend."

He bobbed his head; I guess that was a yes. Then he said, "I'll wait for you to call me, 'cause I'm not gonna call you again."

Okay, I could understand that.

I watched him walk over to his boys, though Troy never just walked—not really. He kinda strutted—like he was a bad boy or something.

Watching him, I couldn't help but grin. But then that went away when Pastor Ford walked into the room. And Zena was with her.

Everybody—except for me—started clapping. So much for my girls having my back. Even India and Veronique were jumping up and down like Zena was something special.

Then, India looked at me and stopped clapping. And like a second later, Troy did the same thing—glanced over and saw me. Stopped clapping right away.

Not that I cared. They could've all kept clapping for an hour—it didn't matter to me. All I did was cross my arms and stare Zena down.

She looked at me and smiled, but then, she was smiling at everybody in the room.

"I guess I don't have to introduce our guest, your mentor," Pastor said, as if all of this was normal. "I just wanted to be here to make the formal introduction."

Yeah, right! That's what Pastor said, but I knew what was up. She was here to make sure I didn't go off like a straight-up fool. I didn't know why everybody was being so careful. I was cool—I'd told them that. This was nothing but business to me.

"Ms. Zena, I am such a big fan of yours," Diamond gushed.

I wanted to put my hand down my throat and throw up.

"Yeah," Arjay added. "You're hot!"

Zena looked at Arjay for an extra second. "You're Anthony's brother."

The way Arjay grinned made me want to put my hands around his neck and choke him. He was supposed to be my friend. All of them—they were all supposed to hate her as much as I did. I knew it was dumb, but it was the truth and I had to tell it.

"I just want all of you to know that I'm the one who's honored," Zena said. "To work with the Divine Divas"—she paused and looked at me and my girls, even though she spent a couple more seconds looking at me—"and the Three Ys Men." Now she looked at the guys. "What a clever name," she added.

I was going to be sick for real this time because now the guys were grinning like Zena had just handed them a million dollars. Even Troy betrayed me.

"I am just delighted to be here, and I'm sure that with all the talent in this room"—she looked at me again—"the Divine Divas are going to be champions."

She raised her arm in the air and cheered, and everybody in the room cheered with her. Everybody except for me.

"Okay, so should we get to work?" Zena asked.

"Before you start," Pastor turned to us, "why don't all of you introduce yourselves."

"I'm Diamond." My girl jumped in Zena's face first. "I hope to be just like you when I grow up."

Zena laughed. "I have a feeling you'll be better than me."

Next was Veronique and India, who just said their names. And then, it was my turn.

I guess everybody thought I was going to let Troy go next, but Zena didn't know me.

So I said, "My name is Aaliyah Reid."

Zena seemed shocked, like she didn't know what to say. "Ah . . . Aaliyah." And then she smiled. "Do you know what your name means?"

Okay, now I was shocked. Why would she ask me that?

She said, "There are many meanings for your name—all wonderful. But the one I love the most, the one that meant the most to me when we were naming you, was 'Highest, most exalted.'" She stopped, as if she wanted to make sure that I understood what she was saying.

"Wow, that's beautiful," Diamond said in a voice that sounded like she was going to cry. Straight-up drama! Diamond might have fallen for that line, but I was smarter than that.

Still, Zena kept on talking. "Your father and I were right on point when we gave you that name."

Everybody stayed quiet. I wanted to ask her why she was telling me this. I wanted to ask her, If you thought I was so exalted, why didn't you stay around? But I didn't say anything because I wasn't about to bring everybody into my business.

The way Zena smiled made me think that she thought I was impressed with that little bit of information. Well, she really needed to just turn around and get gone, because that didn't do anything for me.

Then Zena moved down the line, stopping in front of Troy.

I just kept staring at her—and not in a nice way—until she finished talking to everybody.

Zena turned to Pastor Ford. "Well, I'm ready to get started," she said. "We have a lot of work to do if we're going to win this thing."

I wished that she would stop saying "we." We—the Divine Divas—had gotten all the way to the end of this competition without her. And we—the Divine Divas—were going to win this with or without the great Zena.

She shrugged off this big ole fur sweater she was wearing, which looked ridiculous to me, since it was May. Then she flipped all that weave that was on her head over her shoulders and looked at the piano. She said to Sybil, "I've been looking over the songs you all chose, and they're fantastic." Then she turned to us. "You girls want to join me over here?"

My best friends almost ran across the room while the guys sat on the floor against the wall. I just took my time walking over to Zena—and wishing I was one of the Three Ys Men. Then I wouldn't have to work with her at all.

At the piano, she handed us each the sheet music. I didn't even look up when she handed me my piece.

Pointing to the piano, Zena asked Sybil, "Do you mind?"

"Not at all," Sybil said, sounding as impressed by Zena as Diamond was.

Zena played a couple of chords.

"Wow, I didn't know you could play the piano," Veronique said.

"Uh-huh. I don't get to play often." Her fingers kept dancing across the keys when she looked up at Veronique. "Do you play?"

"The keyboard," she said. Then Zena scooted over on the bench and Veronique sat right down next to her.

I didn't know what Zena's game was, but I was beginning to think that I'd made a mistake by saying I would do this. I wasn't feelin' this at all. Zena was coming in and taking over everything—even my friends.

"Okay." Zena kept talking, even though she was still playing the piano. "Girls, you start singing, and then, as we begin this, I'll let you know where we'll do the solos."

"I cannot believe we are here singing with Zena!"

I rolled my eyes. How many times was Diamond going to say that? But I started singing anyway. Then, after the first stanza, Zena stopped. She looked around at all of us. "Is everyone all right?"

I knew she was talking about me, because I was the only one who was kinda half-singing and half-talking.

But I nodded like everything was fine and then made up my mind to do better, 'cause the better I did, the better we would sound and the sooner I could leave.

"Okay, let's try this again from the top," Zena said.

This time, I sang the song like I meant it, and when we got to the end, Zena said, "My goodness, you girls can really sing."

"You think so?" Diamond asked.

Zena nodded. "And it might be great if you could play the keyboard onstage," she said to Veronique.

"Really? You think so?"

Oh, brother! Veronique was turning into a Diamond mini-me!

Looking down at the sheet music, Zena said, "Now we have to arrange the solos." She stopped and looked at each of us. "I have another surprise that I wasn't going to tell you till next rehearsal." Her grin got even wider. "You know that this go-round you have to sing two songs, right?"

My girls nodded. I didn't.

"Well, the second song . . . you're going to sing with me!"

"You're going to sing with us?" India asked.

Zena nodded, like she was really excited. "Isn't that fabulous?"

"Yes," everyone cheered.

No, I screamed inside.

"And, not only that, each one of you will sing a little duet with me."

"Hold up!" Diamond screamed in her over-the-top way. "I'm going to sing with you by myself?" She held her hand against her chest.

But while Diamond was all about the drama, I felt like I was going to have a heart attack for real. I was going to have to sing with Zena? Stand next to her? Act like I liked her?

No way!

Without saying a word, I turned around. Before any of them knew what had happened, I grabbed my bag and ran right out of there.

"Aaliyah!" Just about everyone was screaming my name, but I heard Pastor Ford the loudest.

That didn't stop me, though. I kept right on going, because the thought of singing with Zena was more than I could take.

Chapter 12

Diamond was doing that hatin' thing again.

She slammed her locker door, and then turned to India. "You better talk to your friend!" Diamond demanded as if I wasn't standing there. As if I wasn't her friend.

"Diamond, you're being stupid," Veronique said.

"No, what's stupid," Diamond waved her finger in the air, "is the way she's messing up everything for us. And if you two don't get your girl in check, she's going to ruin the Divine Divas." Then, as if I suddenly existed, she said to me, "Just get over it."

I watched her stomp away and couldn't believe that she was talking to me like that. At another time, I would've gone all the way off. But I couldn't now, because Diamond had a point. I *was* about to ruin everything.

Right away, India turned to me and gave me one of those looks like she was sorry that Diamond had hurt my feelings. But the only thing that was hurting me was remembering what had happened at rehearsal last night.

It wasn't like I meant to run out of there. It was just that I couldn't take it anymore. The way Zena was falling all over my friends and the way they were falling all over her. And then I broke with that stuff about having to sing with her.

When I ran out of there, I didn't know what I was going to do. But thank God, my dad was waiting right there—as if he had never left. As if he had a feeling that I was going to blow up.

My dad is the coolest, because after I jumped into the car, all he did was take off. He didn't ask me a thing. Even when we got home, the only thing he wanted to know was if I wanted something to eat. But all I wanted to do was go to my room, go to bed, and act like the whole night had never happened.

By this morning, I was sure my dad knew everything, because after we got home last night our phone was blowing up. Everybody was calling him giving the four-one-one on what had gone down.

"Don't let Diamond upset you," Veronique said, making me forget about last night.

I waved my hand like Diamond didn't matter. "I'm not hardly thinking about her."

India and Veronique nodded like they knew what I *was* thinking about. Like they knew my problem wasn't Diamond—it was Zena, who was all up in my head.

Then, all of a sudden, India whispered, "I can't imagine what it would be like not to live with Tova."

Veronique nodded.

India kept on, "I don't know what I would've done if I didn't know her and then all of a sudden she came back."

"It would be tough for me, too." Veronique turned so that she was looking straight in my face. "But here's the thing, my sistah, suppose God brought your mother back to you?"

That was a shocker, 'cause Pastor had said the same thing. "Why would He do that?" I wanted to know what she was thinking.

"I don't know. I don't know everything about God. I just have a feeling that this is a question you should be asking. 'Cause if God did bring your mom back and you keep turning her away, then in a way, aren't you turning away from God, too?"

"That's a good point," India said, kind of excitedly. As if what Veronique said made sense. "Maybe God brought Zena back to you right now because you need her."

This time, I was the one to slam my locker, giving India and Veronique my answer without saying a word.

"Well, whatever you want to do," Veronique began, backing away from her God theory, "you know we got your back, right?"

The way she said that, and the way India kept nodding, made me feel bad about the way I was acting.

And then when India added, "Yeah, 'cause you're way more important to us than any old competition," all I wanted to do was cry.

"Thanks," I said as I hugged India and Veronique. But then I rushed out of school, not waiting to walk to the bus with them. It wasn't like I was mad or anything. I just felt dizzy, like I couldn't get any of my thoughts together.

If only . . . if only . . . if only Zena would go away. But I knew I needed to stop thinking about the if onlys. The if only was never going to happen.

Chapter 13

I don't know why, but I decided to walk home. I guess it was because I didn't feel like seeing anybody, and on the bus, I might see everybody. I needed some me-time and that meant I had to walk, 'cause nobody walked anywhere in Los Angeles.

But by the time I got to the corner of my block, my legs were aching. I guess walking over two miles with a heavy backpack was no joke.

All I wanted to do was get home so I could just chill. I was going to stay by myself and not even call India or Veronique this weekend. I didn't have to worry about Diamond. The way things were going, I wasn't sure my girl would ever call me again.

I was hoping that being by myself would help me figure this whole thing out. And then I thought about Troy. Maybe I *would* call him, 'cause he was the only one who didn't seem to care about Zena. Maybe he could help me. Since he was a guy, he might have some ideas on how to get rid of her.

When I turned into my driveway, I don't think there was ever a time when I was so glad to be home. But then I stopped. I hadn't even noticed my dad's car. This was weird, 'cause he always worked late on Fridays.

I sighed—I knew what this meant. He'd given me a pass last night, but now he'd come home early to talk to me. I was so talked-out.

Maybe I can sneak up to my room. That's what I was thinking when I put my key in the door. I turned the key as slowly as I could so it wouldn't make any noise. If my dad was in his bedroom, I would be able to tiptoe in and up the stairs. If I got to my room, I'd be free and it could be hours before he would even know that I was home.

I squeezed my eyes tight and turned the doorknob. I rose up onto my tiptoes, getting ready to sneak in, but when I opened the door and peeked inside, my feet hit the ground.

Shocker!

Sitting in my living room, in my house, was Zena.

Just a minute ago, all I'd wanted to do was come home. Now all I wanted to do was turn around and run away.

"Hey, sweetheart," my dad said.

The two of them jumped up off the couch at the same time, but only my dad came running over to me. Like he knew that if he didn't get to me quick, I was gonna make my move. Like if he gave me any time, I was gonna cut and run.

"Hi, Daddy," I whispered. I was talking to him, but my eyes stayed right on Zena. She was still standing, still in the same spot as when I had walked in.

I dropped my backpack on the floor, and then my dad took my hand the way he used to when I was a little girl and we were getting ready to cross the street. He always told me to hold his hand so that I wouldn't be in danger. I guess he thought I was in danger now.

Zena didn't say a word until my dad dragged me into the living room and made me stand in front of her.

"Hello, Aaliyah." At least she said that with a smile.

But I didn't say a word; I wasn't fooled. She was only here to tell on me, to get me in trouble for what happened last night. But I could've told her to save her breath. Everybody had already called to give me up.

"Aaliyah," my dad said. "Did you hear—"

Before he could finish, I said, "Hello," in the most polite voice I could. I tried to smile back, but my lips just wouldn't go that way.

But just saying hello seemed to make my dad happy, and that was enough for me.

"Well." My dad sounded like the three of us standing in the living room was a regular thing. "This is good. We all need to sit down and talk."

"Yes," Zena nodded. "I really wish we had done this before."

I knew what she meant. She had wanted to talk to me before the rehearsal last night. As if that would have changed anything.

Zena looked at me as if she was waiting for me to say something, but I didn't have anything good to say and since I was trying to be mature, I said nothing. I wanted Zena to see that my dad had raised me right, even without her.

"So, can we talk?" Zena asked as if she still wasn't sure if I was going to stay. Like she thought I just might find a way to get the heck out of there.

When I nodded, my dad finally let go of my hand.

"Good," Zena said with a great big smile. She moved her hand like she wanted me to sit next to her, but that was when I did turn around and run away. Well, not run away for real; I mean, our living room wasn't that big. But I did walk kinda fast over to the blue chair in front of the window, because that was the only place where I could sit that was far away from her.

I could tell by the way my dad blinked that he didn't

know what to do with me. In a way, I felt a little bad, 'cause my dad was super chill and I never, ever wanted him to be upset with me.

But even though I knew he wanted me to sit next to Zena, sitting in this chair was the best I could do.

My dad finally sat down on the couch next to Zena, and then the two of them just stared. This was so weird that it was hard for me to sit still. The way they were looking at me made me feel like I was in biology and under some kind of microscope.

All I could do was stare back at them—and that was even weirder. This was the first time I had ever seen Zena and my father together. Well, I guess it wasn't exactly the first time, but it was the first time that I could remember.

Sitting here, I couldn't figure out how they ever got together. They looked so different—my dad was just chillin' in a Sean John track suit that I bought him last Christmas. But then there was Zena—all Hollywood, with her long red hair weave that was curled all the way down her back and wearing some kind of pink feather boa that looked like something I would wear for Halloween.

Okay, maybe that was mean. 'Cause I could tell that that boa thing she had wrapped around her neck was expensive. Just like the white button-up sweater, which I could tell was cashmere because I had been shopping with Diamond a million times. And when she was standing up, I saw that she was wearing some True Religion jeans. I hated to admit it—ole-girl looked really nice.

But even though Zena looked good, she didn't look like my mother; she didn't look like my father's wife. Not the way Diamond's parents, Mr. Linden and Ms. Elizabeth, went together. And not even the way India's parents fit—even though her dad was black and her mother was white.

My parents didn't look like a pair at all.

My parents.

Zena said, "I wanted to talk about what happened last night."

I looked at my dad real quick to see if he was mad. His face didn't change, but mine did. See, I knew she only wanted to get me in trouble.

Then she said, "I understand, Aaliyah."

Just as I was ready to get mad and go off, she had to say that.

She said, "I understand how difficult this is for you."

"Yeah, it is," I said out loud. But inside, I was thinking that it didn't take a nuclear physicist to figure that out.

Zena nodded. "Just like you, this is difficult for me." Zena looked down at her hands and I did, too. Even from all the way across the room, I could see that her nails were painted with some kind of sparkly gold polish. Now, that was hot—not that I would admit that to anyone out loud, but Zena did know how to work it.

When she started talking, I put my mad face back on.

She said, "I've so wanted to be part of your life, and this was the only way I could figure out how to do it. How to come back home."

She was trying to sell me, but I wasn't buying anything. If she had wanted to be a part of my life, she could have been. She was rich—she could do anything she wanted to do.

She said, "Now I see that although I had the right intentions, maybe I didn't do this the right way."

You think?

She said, "But that's nothing new. I've made a lot of mistakes."

When she looked at me now, there were tears in her eyes. I hope she didn't expect me to cry with her, because I wasn't going there.

75

It looked like my dad and Zena were waiting for me to say something. But I stayed quiet.

"I know you hate me for what I've done," Zena said. "But you can't hate me as much as I hate myself."

That made me feel a little bad. I mean, I never heard of anybody hating their own self.

"But I'm here, and I really want to help you win this contest."

Okay, now I did have something to say. "I thought you wanted the Divine Divas to win." I didn't want her thinking that she had to do anything special for me.

She blinked and frowned, as if she didn't understand what I was talking about. "That's what I mean—you *and* the Divine Divas. You girls are fantastic, and I have no doubt that you can win this."

"I think we can win, too." It wasn't all about what she thought.

She nodded. "Then we have to find a way to get through this, Aaliyah. You have to let me work with you. Through the rehearsals and . . ." She stopped for a second. "We *are* going to have to sing together." Her voice got softer when she said, "I know that's the part that upset you last night."

She was on point with that. I had tried to push singing with her out of my mind, but the thing was, I did want to win. So I knew I was going to do the Big S and practice with her, sing with her, just handle it.

"So, do you think we can do this?" Zena asked.

I nodded.

"Together?" she asked again.

Now why did she have to go and add that part? It was like she was rubbing it in. But I nodded again.

She let out a deep breath, like she was glad that I agreed. "Great."

"But . . ." And then I stopped.

"But what?"

I looked at her. And then I looked at my dad.

He nodded. "Go on, sweetheart. You can tell us. What were you going to say?"

My eyes went right back to Zena. "But after this is over, you're gonna leave L.A., right?"

She took a deep breath. "Well, I want to do what's best—"

"Don't you have somewhere else to go?"

She looked straight at me when she shook her head. "My plan was that now that I'm back, I'm going to stay . . . for you, Aaliyah."

I was quick to tell her the truth. "You don't have to do anything for me. When this is over, you can leave, because I don't want you to stay."

Her head dropped a little, but my dad just stared straight at me.

"Aaliyah!"

The way he said my name let me know there was trouble.

He said, "You didn't need to say that. You don't get to make those kinds of decisions."

Why was he going off on me? "You were the one who told me to say what I was thinking."

"Don't get smart, young lady."

"I'm not. . . ."

"There's a way we treat people in this house."

Okay—I was not feelin' this. My dad hardly ever went off—that was the first problem. And the second problem was, I didn't want him going off on me like this in front of Zena.

Zena raised her hand and touched my dad's shoulder. "It's okay, Heber. She's just being the way you raised her to be; she's just being honest."

"It's not okay," he said, still staring, still angry.

I couldn't believe this was going down this way. Now I was mad, too.

I jumped out of the chair and said. "Can I go up to my room?" If my father was going to take Zena's side, then I didn't need to be here. They were making all the decisions anyway.

My dad didn't even say anything to me. Just waved his hand, telling me to go on.

I ran past them, grabbed my backpack, and dashed up the stairs. When I got to my room, I wanted to slam the door to let them know just how mad I was, but I wasn't crazy.

I wasn't about to slam any doors—not with the assistant chief of police sitting right downstairs.

Chapter 14

It was like I was frozen to my bed.

Just frozen and just waiting to hear the front door close. But even after a lot of time went by, I didn't hear a thing. Zena was still downstairs, still talking to my dad. I just wanted her to go home—go back to whatever hotel she was staying at.

I could not believe this was happening. My dad was mad at me—all because of Zena.

It was getting harder to sit still; I pushed off the bed and tiptoed to my door. I only opened it a little and peeked into the hallway. Of course, I didn't see anyone, but I could hear a little bit even though my dad and Zena were talking so softly. There was no way, though, for me to really hear what they were saying unless I snuck into the hallway and hung out at the top of the stairs. And I wasn't about to do that. If my dad was mad now, he'd go ballistic if he caught me doing that.

I closed my door as quietly as I'd opened it, then stomped over to my window. This was just some straight-up mess. First Diamond wasn't speaking to me, and now, if Zena stayed downstairs with my dad much longer, he might end up not talking to me either.

I turned back toward my bed and stopped cold. My heart started doing that fast beating thing again before I went over and pulled the box from under the bed.

Zena must've been really getting to me, because I couldn't believe that I had left the box out like this from last week. Whenever I took it out of my closet, I always put it right back; I never, ever let it stay under my bed.

What if Ms. Rachel, the lady who cleaned our house, had found it? That would've been crazy, 'cause as nosey as she was, she would've opened it. And then she would've seen what was inside. And then, she would've told my father. . . .

Thank God that didn't happen.

I went back to my door one more time to check on my dad and Zena before I sat in my rocking chair with the box on my lap. Lots of times, I would take the box out of the closet. But mostly, it was just so I could put something in; hardly ever did I take anything out.

It took a moment to wiggle the top off. And then I just sat there, staring at all the piles and piles of papers.

How weird was this? I was looking at this stuff and Zena was right downstairs.

The cards were on top, and I popped off the rubber band. They were in the order I'd bought them, though the top one was starting to get some of that yellow stuff around the edges.

I opened the first card:

You're the coolest mom
The best one in town
So, that's why we celebrate today
Fun and love all around.

* * *

I rolled my eyes. Every time I read that one, it got cornier and cornier to me. But what did I expect? That was the first card I'd ever bought. It wasn't like I knew that the words inside were all that important.

I mean, I started this when I was like eight years old. I was at the mall—with Diamond (who else?) and her mom—when Diamond dragged us into one of those card stores. It was just a couple of days before Mother's Day, but I hadn't really thought about it, because I didn't have a mother and my dad always bought the cards for my grandmother.

While Diamond and Ms. Elizabeth started looking at cards, I just kinda stood there, 'cause I didn't know what else to do. Then I went to the other side of the aisle where the funny cards were.

It wasn't like I was gonna buy a card, but when I picked one up, for the first time ever, I thought about Zena and how she was a mother, but she didn't have anybody to buy her a card. I don't know why I felt sorry for her, but I did.

So while Diamond and her mom were on the other side, I grabbed a card, then ran over to the cash register. I was so glad there wasn't a long line—I didn't want Diamond or her mother to see me and ask what I was doing.

The lady at the cash register had hair that was so silver it looked like aluminum foil. She pushed some buttons and then said, "Three-fifty."

I remember being so scared when she said that. What had I been thinking? It wasn't like I had any money. All that was in my pocket was the same two dollars my dad had given me that morning.

I closed my eyes, remembering how embarrassed I was that day. . . .

"I said, three-fifty," the aluminum foil lady repeated.

All I wanted to do was run away. But even though I was scared, my feet wouldn't move.

"Do you want this card?" the lady asked me. She sounded like one of my teachers, Mrs. Robinson, who talked like that when she got mad.

But I didn't know what to do. So all I did was nod and kind of whispered, "I want it."

Her eyes got real small when she held out her hand. "Then you have to pay for it. Three-fifty."

I didn't want to cry, but I could feel the tears coming.

Just when I thought I was going to look like a big ole baby, a man in a black suit with a white thing around his neck leaned over to me. "Is that a Mother's Day card for your mom?"

I nodded, because I couldn't talk.

"That's wonderful," he said. Then he stood up straight. "I'll pay for it." He gave the lady four dollar bills.

Even though she had her money, I could tell she was still mad, because she rolled her eyes while she stuffed my card into a bag.

Looking up at the man, I said, "Thank you," and then I got the heck out of there.

When I was outside, I remembered my two dollars and thought I should give it to the man. But I was too scared to go back inside, and I couldn't wait for him because then Diamond and her mom came out and I had to go with them. . . .

I shook my head now as I remembered all of that. I was such a kid then. But in a way, I felt kinda bad, because it's not like I had grown up too much.

The stack of Mother's Day cards in my hand was thick, because every year after that, I went to the store and bought Zena a card. Nobody knew about that—I didn't even tell my BFFL, because I didn't want India to ask why I was buying Mother's Day cards when I didn't even have a mother. It would've been hard to explain to India—or anybody—because I couldn't even explain it to myself.

And I couldn't explain why I was reading these cards right now. But I read every one—including the one I bought for Mother's Day a couple of weeks ago, right before we went to New York.

I wrapped the cards back up, laid them on the floor next to the chair, then looked through all the newspapers and magazines. Every time I saw Zena in something, I saved it. Diamond helped me a lot, even though she didn't know it. She was the one who always had a magazine in her face, and whenever she said anything about Zena, I went out and got the same magazine.

I'd only been doing this for about three years, but now this felt stupid, too. I mean, why did I have pictures of Zena in London and in Japan? Why did I care that she was standing on some kind of stage in South Africa with Nelson Mandela?

I was staring at the pictures when I heard the front door downstairs slam. Jumping up, I ran to my window just in time to see a man holding open the door of one of those long, black, shiny limousines.

Zena bent over to get into the back, but then she stopped. With one leg in the car and one out, she looked up—straight to my window! I couldn't believe it; it was like she knew I was there.

At first, I wanted to jump back. But I wasn't even sure that she could see me with the way the sunlight was on the glass. But then she smiled a little. And then, she waved her hand.

I didn't do anything—didn't smile, didn't wave back. Just stood there. And watched her leave. And wondered if she was going to ever come back. Not that I really cared.

I stood there and watched the driver close her door, then

get into the car himself. I stood there as the car moved real slow into the street. And I even stood there when I couldn't see the limousine—or Zena—anymore.

At first, when I heard the knock on my door, I wanted to roll over and pretend that I was asleep. But I wanted to see my dad. I wanted to know if he was still mad at me.

I sat up on my bed and whispered, "Come in."

My dad walked in, and when he looked at me, he didn't have the smile in his eyes that he always did. But his lips weren't turned down, either, so I guessed that he wasn't straight-up mad, just kinda half mad.

I scooted over on my bed so that he could sit next to me.

He did, but when a couple of minutes passed and he stayed quiet, I wondered if I was wrong about him being mad. Maybe he was so mad that he couldn't even think of anything to say.

I started wishing that I had really been asleep. And then, shocker!

"I'm sorry," he said.

I didn't have any idea what he was apologizing for, but I knew that I did have something to be sorry about. So I said, "Me, too, Daddy. I'm sorry I talked to Zena that way."

"I know you are," he said. "Maybe this is too much for you. I'm asking you to have a relationship with your mother, and maybe it's too soon. Maybe you're just not ready."

I wanted to tell him to stop calling her my mother, but I figured that was really a different subject. Right now, I had some other stuff that I wanted to talk about.

He said, "You've always been so mature."

"I try to be."

He nodded. "I know, but . . ."

Now I felt bad. Like my dad was depending on me and I was letting him down. But there was something I just had to ask him. Something that would help him see my side. Cutting right to it, I asked, "Why aren't you mad at her?"

I thought that was an easy question, but my father didn't say anything for a while. Then, "I was very upset—mad, angry—at Zena for many years. But the thing is, Aaliyah, it wasn't all her fault. I didn't give her a lot of room." He paused and looked down at his hands. "To be honest, I thought I could force her to do it my way." His voice got softer. "I thought I could force her to give up her dreams."

I shook my head. "No matter what," I said, "she should've never left us."

"I don't think she saw it so much as leaving us as finding herself."

"Huh?"

"That's what I've been trying to tell you, sweetheart. This is complicated. Dreams are not always easy to give up, and instead of supporting Zena, I tried to talk her out of what God had put in her heart. And then, when she decided to follow what was inside of her, I didn't give her much of a choice."

"I don't care what you say, Daddy." I folded my arms and pouted, doing that brat thing again. But I *didn't* care about all of that. No matter how many good things he tried to say about Zena, the only thing that counted was that she had gone away.

He kinda chuckled a little, even though I don't think he really saw anything funny. "Oh, to be young again," he said. "So young that you don't even know what you don't know."

Okay—since I was in the third grade, I had gotten all As, but that was too deep for me.

"Life . . . it's just not easy, baby girl. You'll find that out." He stood up and kissed my forehead.

"How am I supposed to just forgive her?"

"Start at that place where God forgives you. And just remember that you're going to make some mistakes, you're going to hurt people that you love."

Nuh-uh.

He said, "And when you do, you're going to want to be forgiven. But don't ask for forgiveness unless you're willing to pass out some of it yourself." He walked toward the door, then stopped. "And that's not a Daddy-thing, that comes straight from God."

Just like Pastor Ford, my dad was playing the God card.

He said, "But one thing you can always count on—if you ever do anything wrong, I will always forgive you. No matter what. And so will God." Then he walked right out of my room, leaving me there to think about him, Zena, and God.

Chapter 15

It felt like everybody had changed their whole lives because of me.

I mean, my dad and I hadn't had anything planned for Memorial Day, but I was sure that Mr. Linden and Ms. Elizabeth had. Diamond's parents were always busy with something—they were always in the newspapers, being photographed at some big party or important meeting. India's father traveled a lot, and Ms. Lena—Veronique's mother—worked all the time. So I just knew everybody else had already had plans for Memorial Day.

The thing was, this was Pastor Ford's party, and even though she had called it at the last minute, everybody was here.

She had only called us on Saturday and told my dad and me that she was having a barbecue for the Divine Divas. At first, I'd been excited. I thought spending the weekend by myself was a good idea, but after the Friday night fiasco with Zena, I needed to have some fun with my girls.

But then, Pastor Ford had told my dad to put me on the

phone, and she'd spoken loud and clear when she'd said that this was a party for the Divine Divas and everybody who was part of the team.

I'd known what that meant.

But I was going to do the Big S—for real this time—especially after the talk I'd had with my dad. I was going to be mature, the way he wanted me to be.

So that's what I was thinking as I was sitting around the edge of Pastor's pool with my girls, Arjay, and Riley. I didn't know what had happened to Troy, but so far it was all cool. Our parents were inside the house, hanging out in the kitchen like they always did. And Diamond was talking and acting like she hadn't been hatin' on me for days.

"It sure is hot out here," Arjay said as he plopped down on one of the overstuffed cushions Pastor Ford had scattered around her pool. He handed Veronique a can of soda.

"What's up with *that?*" Diamond smirked. Even though it was more than eighty degrees, Diamond was the only one wearing a bathing suit—well, just a bikini top. She had on jean shorts, just like me, India, and Veronique.

"What?" Arjay shrugged his shoulders like he didn't have any kind of an idea what Diamond was talking about.

"Is Vee the only one you see sitting here? Or is she the only one who's hot?"

I laughed, but for once, I had to agree with my girl. I mean, I was sure the three wise men in the Bible were gentlemen, so shouldn't our Three Ys Men be the same way? Diamond was right—Arjay should've brought us all sodas.

"Well, Vee is kinda hot," Arjay said, licking his lips.

No, he didn't.

We all laughed; well, we laughed, Veronique kinda giggled. It was amazing to me—since she'd started hanging out with Arjay, she acted more and more like Diamond.

"Men!" Diamond said, then pushed herself up and stomped over to the table, where Pastor had laid out a ton of food.

I got up and followed her—until Zena walked through the sliding glass doors. Then I did a quick about-face and marched the other way. But as I headed back to the pool, India, Riley, Veronique, and Arjay all jumped up and almost knocked me over trying to get to Zena.

But I wasn't going to get mad. Mature, right?

So instead of sitting around and getting an attitude, I just kinda strolled to the other side of the backyard, wishing I had brought a book with me. Then, when one of Pastor Ford's Shiba Inus barked, I stopped and played with the three dogs that were tied up behind a fence.

"So are you a dog girl?"

I had to squint when I looked up, because the sun was in my eyes. It was still hard to see, but I could tell who it was by his voice.

"What's up, Troy?" I said. "You just getting here?"

"Yeah, my dad had something to do this morning." He looked around the backyard. "This is pretty cool," he said, nodding his head like he was giving his approval.

"Yeah, I love Pastor's house."

"You've been here before?"

I nodded. "A lot. She always has us over."

"Wow, that's tight. She's all right for a religious person."

I laughed. "Aren't you a religious person? I mean, you *are* dancing with a group called the Divine Divas. And this *is* a gospel competition."

"So what are you asking me?"

"Well, you said Pastor was religious and I wanted to know if you were, too."

"See, I knew it!" He laughed.

I frowned. "What?"

"You been playin' all hard to get and everything. I knew that you were interested in me."

"What're you talking about?"

"Just admit it." He leaned closer and lowered his voice. "You're into me. Just say it; it'll be all right, Pretty Lady."

If any other guy had stepped to me with those sorry lines, he would've gotten his feelings hurt. But the way Troy was grinning, I knew he was kidding. At least, I hoped he was.

So I just laughed. And he laughed with me. Until I turned around and peeped everyone still hanging on to Zena like she was something special.

Troy looked over to where all the guys were, too, and I just knew he wished he was over there hanging out with Zena.

"You can go on," I said. I didn't want him to feel like he had to hang with me. I could do fine all by myself.

He turned back to me and looked like he hadn't heard what I'd said. "What?"

"I know you want to go over there and talk to Zena. So go ahead."

He frowned. "I don't wanna talk to her. I wanna talk to you."

My voice went down kinda low when I said, "You don't have to." I didn't know why I was feeling so bad all of a sudden. I mean, I wasn't mad at my girls for hanging all over Zena; I'd gotten used to them. It was just that Troy was different. He was the only one who wasn't into her—at least not until now. By the way he looked at me, I knew what was coming next.

He said, "Let's get out of here. Go for a walk around the block. We can see if Pastor will let us take the dogs out."

Shocker! I thought Troy wanted to be with Zena. But all he wanted to do was hang with me. I felt like Troy was coming to my rescue, the same way Arjay had rescued Veronique in New York. The only thing was, he wasn't rescuing me from a pervert—only from Zena.

As much as I wanted to go, I knew I had to stay.

"Nah, we'd better not."

" 'Kay. Maybe later."

Before I could say anything else, Zena came over to us.

"Hi, Troy," she said.

"What's up?"

That was all he said. He treated her like she was just a regular ole person.

Then she turned to me. "The best for last." She smiled. "How're you, Aaliyah?"

"I'm good."

I had to push my legs into the ground to stop myself from running away from her. Especially since I could feel everybody watching us. Just standing back, like I was on stage or something. Everybody except for Troy; he just stayed right next to me. As if he really did want to rescue me if I needed him to.

Zena looked around the backyard. "This is some place Pastor Ford has."

"Yeah, it's cool," I said.

"I'm so glad she arranged this barbecue for us."

"Yeah, I'm glad."

"Gives us all a chance to get to know one another."

"Yeah, it does."

I guess Zena got tired of all of my answers sounding the same, because then she said, "Is your father here? I didn't see him when I came in."

"Yeah, he's inside." I was going to just stop there, but something made me say, "He's in there with all the *other* grown-ups."

Everybody got quiet. I didn't mean for that to come out the way it sounded—as if I wanted her to go hang with people her own age. But she didn't seem upset. Just kinda smiled and nodded. Said, "I'll be back."

It wasn't until she walked away that I started breathing again. Then Troy turned to me, and instead of saying something about Zena, he said, "You want a soda?"

"Yeah, thanks."

But what he did next was the real shocker—he took my hand, squeezed it, and strutted away as if nothing had happened. And when he turned his back to me, all I could do was smile.

I had no idea how we ended up like this—like couples. Well, almost.

First, there was India and Riley, sharing one of the oversized chairs Pastor had in the backyard. Veronique and Arjay were sitting side by side on the edge of the pool. And then, there was me and Troy. And Diamond. Diamond and I both stood behind Troy, watching his thumbs move faster than a speeding bullet as he played Arjay and Riley on their PlayStations.

"Oh, you got me," Arjay screamed out.

Troy laughed and Diamond and I laughed, too. I never knew what the big deal was with this PlayStation thing, because for me, I'd rather be reading a book. But now it did seem kind of cool. With all the different games—and Troy showed me that you could watch movies on it, too—I started thinking that maybe I would ask my dad for one for my birthday that was coming up.

The guys had started playing after we'd finished eating, and they hadn't stopped. But the thing was, I wasn't bored, like I usually was after a couple of hours of just hanging out. I was all into it today. Truth—I wasn't sure if it was the game or Troy.

There was only one word I could think of to describe him, and I hated that it was one of Diamond's words, so old-school. But Troy was fierce. I mean, he was winning every game. And he was so cool about it. He never jumped up and down or talked trash. It didn't matter if they were kickboxing or doing that race car thing; Arjay and Riley couldn't get anywhere near Troy.

Yup, Troy was fierce. And really nice, though I didn't want anybody to get it twisted—I wasn't thinking about him like that.

The guys were in the middle of another game when we heard the sliding glass door open. But no one looked up until we heard her voice.

"I got next."

We all turned around. And looked. And stared at Zena.

She had next? What was she talking about?

"What're you guys playing?" she asked.

"I don't think you want any of this, Ms. Zena," Arjay said, kinda laughing.

"First of all"—she put her hands on her hips—"do not call me *Ms.* Zena." She leaned closer to all of us and whispered, "I'm too young for that."

I think she wanted us to laugh, but only Diamond did. The rest of them smiled, and I just looked at her like she was crazy.

"And then second." Now she was talking regular. "I know a lot about those games. There was one in the gift bag last year when I sang at the Grammys, and I got hooked right away."

That impressed Diamond, 'cause she said, "Oh, my God, you've been to the Grammys?" Now it was Diamond who I looked at like she was crazy. Everybody knew Zena had been to the Grammy's a million times. Diamond—especially—knew everything about Zena.

Then, Diamond started stuttering, "I mean . . . I know . . . you've been there . . . but, it's just kinda amazing that you're here . . . right now . . . talking to us about . . . the Grammys. Oh, my God." She started holding her chest—like always.

While they all laughed, I rolled my eyes. Straight-up drama!

"Yeah, I've been to a couple of those shows," Zena said before she squatted down and sat on one of those thick pillows. I hadn't thought any of the grown-ups would come out here and sit with us—let alone sit on one of those pillows.

Zena kept talking like being around us was no big deal. "And I'm telling you, the best gift I ever got was one of those PlayStations."

"So, you actually play?" Arjay asked.

She smiled and nodded. "Like I said, I got next."

"Ooohhh, I think she's calling you out," Veronique kidded.

"Yeah!" India laughed. "So what you gonna do?" She was looking straight at Riley.

Riley looked from Arjay to Troy. At first, neither of them said anything, then Arjay piped in, "You know what, Ms.—I mean, Zena. Here," he said, standing up. "Take mine. Let's see if you're any good, 'cause my boy here," he patted Troy on the back, "never loses."

"Yeah," Riley said, putting his game down. "You can play Troy."

"Oh, you scared, huh?" Zena teased. I couldn't believe she was acting like this. I mean, she was so much older—Troy was gonna kill her.

Zena grabbed Arjay's game. "Well, let's see how good you are, Mr. Troy." She looked at him and made a funny face—like she was about to go to war. "What's it gonna be?"

He just shrugged, as if sitting in the backyard and playing the world-famous Zena was no big deal. I was really feelin' Troy; he was as unimpressed with Zena as I was.

When Troy looked at Zena and said, "This is your drama, you pick the game," I liked him even more.

Zena picked the race car game, which, from what I could tell, was one of the most popular, and hardest, games.

Troy nodded, and then they began.

It wasn't like I really understood the game, but as I sat next to Troy, I started to get into it. Everybody was into it, cheering, jumping up and down, making all kinds of noises—for Zena.

To me, that was cold. Troy was our guy, but they were all acting like Zena was their best friend. It didn't matter to me that my friends were traitors. I stood behind Troy and rooted for him as if I would get a million dollars if he won.

After about five minutes, Arjay covered his mouth with his fist and let out a howl. Riley gave him a high five, and the two jumped around.

I wasn't sure what was going on, but with the way Zena was smiling, I had a bad feeling.

Zena laid Arjay's game down on the concrete, then stood up and jumped around with her hands in the air like she was some kind of boxer or something.

"I can't believe that," Arjay howled some more.

Diamond, India, and Veronique were laughing and cheering, too. I was the only one who was quiet—well, me and Troy.

I couldn't believe it—Zena had really beaten him? Even though I was close to him, I didn't want to look at Troy's face. I mean, if it had been me, I would've been stone-cold mad right about now. But then, shocker! I peeked at Troy and he was grinning.

He stood up, leaving me on the other side of the pool by myself, and walked over to Zena.

Holding out his hand, he said, "Gotta give it to you, Ms. Z, you're the first one to ever beat me like that."

She shook his hand. "Well, I had to show you a little something, right?"

"Yeah, but I want a rematch."

"You got it. Maybe later."

I was the only one in the backyard who hadn't moved. All the rest of them were still around Zena—and now even Troy seemed to be all into her.

Truth—I couldn't really hate on Zena all that much. I mean, look at what she'd done—as old as she was, she'd just beaten Troy.

That was off the chain. Really. At least, it really would have been. If it had been anybody but Zena.

Zena turned toward the house, and they all followed her like she was the Pied Piper. Not one of them turned back. Not even my BFFL was thinking about me. It was like I wasn't even here anymore.

I turned around and just as I started walking back over to Pastor Ford's dogs, I heard footsteps behind me. It was Troy, coming back to the pool—to pick up his game, I guessed. But he circled around and stopped in front of me. Held out his hand and asked, "You coming?"

Someone had remembered me. And for some reason, I was really glad that someone was Troy.

"Yeah," I said and took his hand.

"Good, 'cause I want you to remember that I got you. Always. Okay?"

I smiled. And nodded.

Because what else could I do?

Chapter 16

It wasn't so bad working with Zena.

I mean, I was still doing the Big S, but at least now I didn't want to run out every time she came into a room.

After the barbecue on Monday at Pastor's house, we'd only met with Zena and Sybil one time, because we were all studying for finals. But three times last week, Zena had called my father and asked to speak to me, just to say hello and wish me luck on my tests. (She must not have known that I didn't need luck—I was blessed.) But anyway, I never talked to her for more than a minute—I wasn't tryin' to do the daughter thing with her. The best she was going to get from me . . . was maturity.

But like I said, this wasn't bad, because Zena wasn't just having us sing—she was teaching us stuff, and I loved that part.

We were all sitting in chairs in the learning center, and Zena had one of the maintenance guys bring in a big blackboard.

"Ms. Z," Diamond said, calling her by the name that everyone called her now—everyone except for me. I just called her Zena. "Are we going to get to sing today? I'm getting a little nervous."

"Why?"

"Because we missed all last week and you know those other groups are practicing."

Zena said, "Sweetheart, the first thing you must learn about being a great singer is not to worry about anyone else. Don't even think about other people. When you're the best that you can be, nothing else matters. That's what's called confidence."

Diamond smiled. "Oh, I got plenty of that."

"You got that right," Troy yelled out.

Zena said, "Good, because you all are going to need that."

Even though we were just practicing singing right now, Zena had told the guys that she wanted them to be at every rehearsal, too. At first, that didn't make sense to me since the guys didn't do any singing, just dancing. But then she explained that if the guys knew everything we knew, we'd be more cohesive. I kinda liked that word, liked that thought.

"Anyway," Zena began. She was smiling, but clearly she wanted to get back to work. "The best way to get started is to learn about singing."

"Learn about singing?" Veronique asked as if that didn't make sense to her, not that it made a lot of sense to me, either. "Don't we just need to know the song? I mean"— Veronique looked around at all of us—"we can all sing."

When Zena said, "A little," the guys busted up laughing.

Oh, no she didn't! I couldn't believe that she just dissed my girl like that. Truth—we *could* sing. More than a little, or else we wouldn't have gotten this far. Zena needed to recognize.

But Zena said, "What I mean, Vee, is that it's clear you girls can sing. But I want to turn you into singers."

That didn't make a lot of sense, and the way my girls were frowning, too, let me know they were with me.

"Let me explain," she said. "Singing is a skill based on muscle memory. It's a form of speech."

Okay, now this was getting interesting. It was starting to sound like something from one of my science classes.

"There are three things you need to know about singing. The first, I'm sure you've heard before." She wrote on the board and spoke at the same time, "You have to breathe properly—from the diaphragm." She faced us again. "Where is your diaphragm?"

Not one of my girls—or the guys—raised their hands. Dang, my friends didn't know anything. Even though I didn't want to, I couldn't help it. I raised my hand.

Zena nodded, and I stood up as if I was in school.

"It's right here," I said, pushing my fingers against my stomach, right above my belly button.

She smiled. "Exactly," she said. She looked at me the way my dad always did—like she was proud. But I wanted to tell her to keep that to herself. She didn't have anything to do with me being smart.

"Everybody stand up," she said. And then she told them to touch their stomachs the way I did. "You're going to sing from there."

"Hold up," Arjay said. "From all the way down there? I thought you sang from your throat."

Zena shook her head as she motioned for us to sit down. "That's what most people think. And that's why most people can only sing"—she stopped and looked at Veronique—"a little."

We all kinda laughed—a little.

"I'm going to teach you how to sing like singers do."

Zena went on to tell us a whole bunch of other stuff. Like

how we had to sing with power, or resonate. How important it was to enunciate. And how we needed to drink lots of water because our voices were like instruments that had to be lubricated and taken care of.

"But here's the last thing," she said. "Do you know the best way to become a great singer?" She looked around at all of us. And then my girls and the guys looked at me. Like I was supposed to know everything.

But I didn't know the answer to that one, so I just looked straight ahead.

Zena smiled. "It's one word . . . practice. So, let's get started."

"Ah, man," Arjay shouted. "That was a trick question."

We all laughed. Diamond was the first to jump right up and take two giant steps to the piano. For me, I was kinda sorry the class part was over. I had learned a lot—there was so much more to singing than just opening your mouth. I was surprised at how much Zena knew and how good she was at teaching us.

I took the sheet music she handed to me when I got to the piano and said, "Thank you."

Zena paused for a moment and smiled like she always did. But this time, her smile seemed a little different. Like it was just for me. And like she had a feeling that I was thanking her for more than just the music.

Truth—I was.

This was the best practice I'd ever had with the Divine Divas because I really liked the classroom part. When my girls and I did some of the things that Zena told us to do—like singing from deep inside, using our diaphragms—we sounded better than we ever had before. I had to give it to her; Zena knew her stuff. And even though I would never say this out loud to anyone, I was starting to be glad that she was our mentor. I mean, were the other mentors teaching their groups how to be real singers?

But then she had to go and ruin everything.

Zena walked over to where I was stuffing my water bottle into my bag. "Good job, Aaliyah," she said so softly that I almost didn't hear her.

"Thanks." I talked just as quietly as she did. I mean, yeah, I liked it when teachers told me how well I was doing, but I didn't want to be called out by Zena like that. Every time she talked to me, everybody stopped and watched us like we were the main attraction in a circus or something.

Zena stayed by my side, but she didn't say anything for a moment. And then, shocker! "Let me give you a ride home."

"No!" I almost screamed. It wasn't like I was trying to be rude, but there was no way I was riding with her. The look in her eyes made me feel kinda sorry, though. So, I said, "I mean, I always ride with Diamond."

And then, my girl—the one who was supposed to be one of my best friends—said, "That's okay, Aaliyah. If I had the chance to rock that limo, I would. You should go with your mom!"

Now see, I wanted to kill Diamond. First of all, I was tired of trying to tell these people that Zena wasn't my mother. And second of all, no matter what I said or did, Diamond was supposed to have my back. Just like I always had hers—even when she made me mad. We were supposed to be the ride-or-die girls. The when-I-roll-you-roll girls.

Zena looked at me like she had new hope in her eyes. As if she really thought I was going to get in a car with her without someone holding a gun to my head. That wasn't going to happen; but I didn't really know how to tell her that.

Then my BFFL said the right thing, the ride-or-die thing. "Aaliyah, remember, you have to ride with us so that we can talk about what we're going to wear in Miami."

"Yeah," Veronique added to India's lie. "Diamond has some pictures she wants us to look at."

Diamond frowned. "No, I . . ." Veronique slapped her arm and Diamond shut up.

Okay, my girls weren't the best liars, but they were all I had right now.

Turning to Zena, I said, "I forgot. I have to ride with them." I felt kinda bad for the way India and Veronique had lied for me, but I wasn't feeling bad enough to tell the truth. Still looking at Zena, I shrugged, said, "Sorry," then grabbed my bag and got the heck out of there. I didn't want to see the look on Zena's face, 'cause it was clear that story India started and Veronique finished was just a big ole lie.

Zena's limousine, which took up almost the whole curb in front of the church, was sitting right in front, and I ran past it, straight into the parking lot. I didn't stop running until I got to Diamond's Honda. I stayed right there and didn't move until all my girls came out just a few minutes after me.

Nobody said anything until we were all inside the car. Then Diamond piped up, "Okay, so does somebody want to tell me what's up? I mean, why wouldn't you want to ride home in style?" she asked, looking at me through the rearview mirror.

I shook my head but didn't say anything. There was nothing for me to say because Diamond would never get it. And truth—I wasn't all that sure that India or Veronique got it either. The only difference between them and Diamond was that India and Veronique had my back better than Diamond did.

Diamond kept on, "If Zena asked me to ride with her, I

would've said, 'See ya,' and one of you divas would've been driving this car home. Trust that."

Veronique said, "Please! You would never let anyone drive this car."

"What are you tryin' to say? You know I share everything. The only reason we have the Divine Divas is because of me. I found the contest and brought my crew right with me."

"Yeah, but I'm not talking 'bout that. . . ."

I was so glad that Veronique had turned everything around to Diamond's favorite subject—herself. While the two of them argued up front, I just looked out the window, thinking about Zena. Why did she have to ask me that? And in front of everybody! Just because I was being nice didn't mean that I wanted to start acting like her daughter. No. I just wanted to get through this competition so that I could go on with my life and she could move on with hers, too. I was going to have to find a way to make Zena—and everybody—catch that clue and understand.

Even though I was sitting in the back of this car with my three best friends, I felt like I was all by myself. Like there wasn't anybody in the world who would ever be able to understand me.

Then my BFFL took my hand. India smiled when I looked at her. And I smiled right back.

All of a sudden, I didn't feel so alone.

Diamond said, "Well, whatever," bringing the subject back to me, "if you don't want to ride with Zena, Aaliyah, then it's your choice, your life." She talked to me through the rearview mirror again.

"That's right," I said. "It is my life."

"You know what," Diamond began as she rolled the car to a stop in front of my house. She turned around and pointed her finger at me. "I was gonna tell you what we were planning for your birthday, but now I'm not gonna say a thing."

She was trying to sound all mad and stuff, but she wasn't hardly upset. With the way India and Veronique were grinning, I could tell that they'd already been talking about what we were going to do on Saturday.

"So, just get out of the car." Diamond waved her hand like she was dismissing me. "So that we can talk about you behind your back."

Even though she was being smart, I had to laugh with her. I mean, what she'd just said—that really was funny.

"Peace," Diamond yelled from her window as she drove away.

I stood in front of my house, waving until I couldn't see the car anymore. What had I been thinking? I wasn't hardly alone. As long as Diamond, India, and Veronique were in my life, I would never be by myself.

They were my ride-or-die crew for real.

Chapter 17

"Where's India?" I asked Veronique.

"Diamond's giving her a ride home because Drama Mama has some new magazines and you know Diamond has got to get her hands on those."

I laughed when Veronique called India's mom Drama Mama; Diamond *had* come up with the perfect name for her. And if anyone knew drama, it was Diamond.

"So they left already?" I asked.

Veronique nodded. "You're stuck with just me, my sistah."

I sucked my teeth and hit Veronique upside her head like I was mad, but I was just playing. And anyway, nobody could hurt Veronique by hitting her through all that hair on her head. "Don't say that; I'm not stuck with you."

I *was* surprised that India had left me without saying anything, but truth—I was kinda glad to be with Veronique. She was one of my favorite people, but I never spent that much time alone with her—it was always the four of us, or just me and India. Now I'm not saying that India wasn't my girl—my

BFFL was the real deal, straight-up. But Veronique was special, too. I didn't know anybody—besides myself—who just told it! It didn't matter what Veronique was thinking, she always told you the truth.

I closed my locker and looked around the hallway as all the other kids pushed by us, but nobody seemed to be in a big hurry. I guess that's because exams were over and tomorrow was the last day of school. Living was easy now.

"Who you lookin' for?"

"Huh?" When I looked at Veronique, she was just grinning away.

"If you're looking for Troy," she said, "he's with Arjay. They're hanging with Arjay's brother. He's supposed to be showing them some steps—he's one of Zena's dancers, remember?"

"Oh, yeah," I said. Arjay had told us a long time ago about his brother. "But I wasn't looking for Troy."

"Stop lyin'!" Veronique said.

My eyes got real big when she said that, but that didn't stop Veronique from talking.

She said, "I don't know why you frontin' like that, 'cause you can't fool me, my sistah. Everybody can see that you got a thing for Troy. And he definitely got a thing for you."

See, that's what I was talking about. Veronique just told it! But this time, she was tellin' it wrong. I wasn't going to say anything, though, 'cause she wouldn't have believed me.

"If you don't see Troy in school tomorrow," Veronique said as we walked through the crowd and down the school steps, "you'll definitely see him on Saturday for your birthday." She looked at me with this big ole grin.

"So, what're we gonna do?" I asked all innocently, knowing already that she wasn't about to tell me.

"Please! You gotta step to me better than that if you wanna

get the four-one-one." Veronique rolled her eyes. "Just know, it's gonna be big—the way we always do. Trust and know."

That was true. Every year, we planned each other's birthday surprises, though for Diamond, we always did the same thing—we went to her favorite restaurant and ordered a special cake. Of course, we had to buy a gift, too—the more expensive, the better—because it was Diamond.

For the rest of us, we usually did something like go to Magic Mountain or hang out at the beach if it wasn't too cold. No matter what, it was always fun.

"I'm kinda excited about Saturday."

"Yeah, it's gonna be ridiculous." And then Veronique stopped talking and started walking slower.

I frowned. "What's up?" I asked. I was more than a little bit concerned. It wasn't hard to see that Veronique had something she wanted to talk to me about.

I began to wonder if this was about her mother . . . or her mother's boyfriend. A little while ago, her mother had kicked her boyfriend, Dwayne, out of the house for trying to kiss Veronique. He had tried to kiss up on her a couple of times, and I was praying inside that she wasn't about to tell me that he was back.

When we got to the bench in front of the bus stop, Veronique sat down. Even though I was kinda worried, it didn't matter what Veronique had to tell me. She was my girl, and whatever she needed, I was ready to ride. And I knew Diamond and India would have her back, too.

She said, "I just wanted to tell you that I know what you're going through."

Huh? It took me a moment to figure out what she was talking about, and when I realized what she was saying, I had to stop myself from getting mad. Why did everybody always want to talk about Zena? There was no way Veronique could know what I was going through. And I really was a little mad that she would even say that.

Before I could tell her that I didn't want to talk about Zena, she said, "Remember, I've lived my whole life without my father."

Okay, I had to sit back and chill for a moment on that. I sat down next to her, but I didn't say a word.

Of course, I'd always known that Veronique didn't know her father—especially with that mess she had gotten into in New York, where she'd met someone on the Internet who was supposed to have introduced her to her dad. As if a stranger would really help you like that.

But the thing was, Veronique had fallen for that lie because she'd so wanted to know her dad. She'd gone through a lot to find him, and, as I thought about it, I began to wonder; maybe she did know what I was going through.

Veronique was staring straight ahead, not looking at me. Like she was in some kind of trance or something. She said, "Here's the thing, my sistah: I would do anything for my dad to just show up one day. For him to come back to me." She stopped, and, still looking across the street, she added, "At least your mother came back."

I was trying to feel Veronique and hear everything she was saying, but our situations were totally different. She wanted her father; I didn't want my mother.

A slow-moving bus finally stopped in front of us, but neither one of us moved. We just watched people get off, people get on, and then we watched the bus pull away.

I knew what Veronique was tryin' to say, but just like she had to speak her truth, I had to tell her mine. "It's too late for me and Zena. Too late for her to try to be my mother."

"No, it's not." Veronique twisted around and faced me for the first time. "It would only be too late if one of you were in a coffin."

My eyes and mouth opened wide. I couldn't believe she'd said that.

And if that wasn't enough, she told me this horrible story. "You know, my cousin Benny never, ever met his father. The first time he saw him face-to-face was when he looked down at him. When his father was dressed in a navy blue suit and about to be put six feet under."

Dang! She was talking straight, but this wasn't what I wanted to hear. I mean, who wanted to talk about funerals? And the way she was saying it, I could imagine the whole thing—the flowers and the sad music and the preacher. I closed my eyes and felt like this cold chill.

I guess Veronique didn't think she had scared me enough, because she kept right on talking. "See, here's the thing, Aaliyah. That's not going to happen to you. You'll never have to worry about seeing your mother for the first time at her funeral." Then tears came to her eyes when she said softly, "But it might happen to me."

She started crying for real. And so did I.

"Vee, that's not going to happen," I said, putting my arms around her and trying to sniff back my tears. "After the contest is over, we're gonna all work together to find your father," I promised, knowing that when I told Diamond and India about this, they'd be with me. And the guys, too. "And Pastor will help. And then, you know my dad will, too." She was still crying, looking like she didn't believe any of this was really going to help.

I added, "We can find your father, trust that. You know Diamond doesn't call my dad Top Cop for nothing."

She laughed a little bit, even though tears were still coming out of her eyes.

When I hugged Veronique again, I felt so bad. I could tell just by the way she was holding me tight that not knowing her father had really hurt her. Just like not knowing Zena had hurt me.

All this time, I'd been feeling sorry for myself, thinking that nobody understood me. Thinking that Zena coming back was the worst thing that could ever have happened.

But Veronique had just told me the truth. Just like my dad had the other night. There were blessings in every situation.

I would just have to work real hard to find the blessing in mine.

Chapter 18

I looked down at my toes, with the bright red polish that matched my manicure.

"Now, see, that's what I'm talking about," Diamond said, holding up her hand and looking at her own manicure. She had gold polish that kinda glittered, just like the kind that Zena wore all the time. "This is beyond fierce!"

I giggled when I looked at Diamond. With that mud mask on her face, she looked like a racoon. I had the same stuff on me, so I didn't know what I was laughing about.

Leaning back in my spa chair, I closed my eyes, but only for a moment, because India said, "That color looks better on you than it does on me." She looked from my toes to hers. "Maybe I should've done what Vee did."

I peeked over at Veronique, who looked more ridiculous than all of us. Because not only did she have that clay on her face but she also had cucumbers covering her eyes. Like she was a diva or something.

India whined, "I should have gotten clear, like Vee."

"Nah," Diamond. "Color is better. And that red looks good on you," she assured her. "Have a little confidence."

I laughed when India rolled her eyes at Diamond. Diamond must've forgotten who she was talking to. The old India was gone, and this new one—well, she didn't take nothing from nobody.

Yeah, my girl used to have a confidence problem, but that was a long time ago. In the past couple of months, my BFFL had changed the most. First, she'd lost a lot of weight, although that one time when I'd caught her throwing up in the bathroom, I'd wanted to slap her silly. But then she'd gone straight. And even though she had gained some of that weight back, I think India finally knew that she was really pretty—no matter how much she weighed. And anyway, India always looked good, because she was the only one of us carrying any real booty.

Plus, she was hanging hard with Riley—like boyfriend, girlfriend hard. India told me her mom wouldn't let her call Riley her boyfriend, which was straight-up ridiculous. Like that was going to stop India. And Riley. Parents just didn't get it, because no matter what you called it, India and Riley were a couple. They were together all the time—just like Veronique and Arjay.

Diamond said to India, "You need to find your inner Tova and be more like your mother. She's confident all the time."

"And you need to sit back and chill, Diamond. And stay out of a conversation that wasn't meant for you."

"Hey!" I said, snapping my fingers in the air.

Diamond said, "I was just sayin' . . ."

India didn't let her finish. "And I was just sayin' that I liked Vee's mani and pedi better. It didn't have a single thing to do with confidence."

"All right," Diamond pouted. "You don't have to catch an attitude."

See, that's what I was talking about. A couple of months ago, Diamond would have walked all over India. Now India was the one doing all the walking and talking.

This time when I leaned back, I closed my eyes. My birthday was starting out tight—an afternoon at the spa was so cool.

My girls still hadn't told me anything when they'd picked me up this morning. And then Diamond had driven us all here—to the Beverly Hills Day Spa.

This place was off the chain. We had a private room, with four massage spa chairs. And while we got manicures and pedicures and facials, they fed us all kinds of fruit and cheeses with sparkling cider.

This had to be Diamond's idea; it was so over the top. But I wasn't hardly complaining. Truth—this was great. Though I'd been a little surprised (and maybe even a little disappointed) when we had pulled up to the spa. I mean, I'd thought we were gonna do something with the guys. That's what Veronique had said the other day. But having this spa day was all good.

"Okay," Diamond said loudly, waking me up from what I was thinking. "We've got to get out of here for the big event."

I frowned a little. "What else are we going to do?" I couldn't imagine doing anything more. I was sure the cost of this was enough.

"None of your business Miss-Nosey-Birthday-Girl."

I rolled my eyes at Diamond, but you better believe I wasn't mad. How could I be? Today I was sixteen, and after this spa experience, I felt like it, too.

It took the women in the spa another hour to get us all presentable enough to leave. And that was when things got really weird. As soon as we got into Diamond's car, India gave me a mask.

"Put this on," she demanded, sounding a little bit like Diamond.

"Why? What is this?"

"Oh, come on, Aaliyah," Diamond whined. "Why do you have to know everything? We're trying to give you a surprise."

After I put it on, Diamond said, "Make sure she doesn't peek."

I only did it because it was my birthday and I didn't want to fight with my girls right now. But I can't say that I was feeling riding around in a car without knowing where I was going.

My girls were whispering like there was still some planning going on or something they didn't want me to hear. I didn't know what the big deal was. We were probably just going to some restaurant. This had to be another one of Diamond's ideas—straight-up drama!

But after a while, I just sat back. Diamond was right. This wasn't a test or anything—I didn't have to know every-thing.

Finally the car stopped, and when I put my hands up to take off the mask, India screamed, "No!"

So I just played along and let India hold my hand while we got out of the car. She didn't let go as we walked and then stopped. I heard a doorbell ring.

Okay, we weren't at a restaurant.

When the door opened, I could hear some whispers, but I kept right on playing along. I could tell we weren't inside my house—I was guessing we were at Diamond's or India's.

Then Diamond said, "Okay now."

Before I could get the mask off my eyes, I heard a roaring kind of shout.

"Surprise!"

Well, I can't say that I was surprised. I mean, I knew I would have some kind of surprise once I took this mask off. But I wasn't expecting this surprise—a surprise party!

We were in someone's family room, in a house I'd never been in before. But it was beautiful, with two walls that were just windows and flowers and plants everywhere around the white leather furniture.

The best part was all the people—Arjay, Riley, and Troy, and then lots of other kids from school. Diamond's mother and father and India's mom. I even recognized Arjay's parents. And Pastor Ford.

My dad was the first one to hug me. "Happy birthday, sweetheart."

I couldn't believe he was here. I mean, this morning, when Diamond had come to pick me up, my father hadn't said a word. All he'd done was tell me that he would see me later— I'd thought that meant later tonight.

"Thanks, Daddy," I said, hugging him back. "I can't believe you knew about this and didn't say anything."

He laughed but didn't get a chance to say anything else, because everybody kinda bum-rushed me. I couldn't even keep up with all the hugs and everyone wishing me happy birthday.

"Welcome to our home," Mrs. Lennox, Arjay's mother, said to me. "And happy birthday, dear."

"Oh, I didn't know where I was." I laughed. "This is your house?"

She nodded.

"Thanks for having me," I said, kind of surprised that the party was here. I'd only met Arjay's parents while we'd been in New York, and they hadn't really hung out with everyone else all that much. When I first saw them, I remember thinking

115

that his parents moved around like a king and queen. There was something about them that made them look like they should be living in a castle.

Arjay's mother smiled. "When Arjay told us that this was *your* sweet sixteen birthday, we wanted to help him do something special." She squeezed my hand. "We were glad to open our home for you."

When I leaned over to hug her (because she was like three inches shorter than me), Arjay came up behind her.

"Hey, you," I said to him. "Thanks for the party."

He kissed my cheek, and then put his arm around his mother's shoulder. "This was all Moms. Thank her."

"She already did, dear." And then she smiled at me some more—like she really liked me, which was cool.

"Yeah, I thanked your mom, and now I'll thank you." I kissed him on the cheek.

"Oh, isn't that sweet?" His mother was grinning like me kissing Arjay was the nicest thing she'd ever seen.

"Yeah, you're sweet, but you better not let Vee see you hittin' on me like that." Arjay and I laughed, but Ms. Lennox didn't. She wasn't even smiling anymore. Really, she looked kinda mad.

Okay, I got it; she didn't like Veronique. I didn't know why, but it was a good thing I was raised to show respect, or else I would've said something to her about the way she was dissin' my girl. I was just glad that Veronique hadn't seen what had gone down. And Arjay? He didn't seem to notice . . . or care. I didn't know which.

But before I could find Veronique to ask her if she knew what was up, Troy rolled over to me.

"Hey." I couldn't stop grinning. I don't know why, but he always made me smile.

But Troy didn't say a word. Just took my hand and pulled

me away from Arjay and his mother. Pulled me away from everyone in that room. Took me around a corner where no one could see us.

I guess he had been to Arjay's house before, 'cause he acted like he knew where he was going.

"What's up?" I said when we stopped walking.

"I couldn't wait anymore."

"For what?"

"For this." And then, shocker! He kissed me. I mean, he straight-up kissed me! On the lips.

It was a quick kiss. Nothing bad. It was all good.

It happened so fast, I didn't even close my eyes. But when Troy leaned back and opened his eyes, all he did was smile and say, "Happy birthday, Pretty Lady." Then he walked away and left me standing there by myself, thinking that was the best birthday gift I'd received in a long, long time.

Even though it was only about three o'clock in the afternoon, this felt like a nighttime party. After all the grown-ups wished me a happy birthday, they all went into the backyard and left us kids alone.

This was straight-up cool; Arjay's parents had hired a DJ, who had this huge screen with him. He showed the videos while he played the songs. We were having a blast, singing and dancing like Beyoncé and Rihanna, and we even pulled some old-school moves with Mary J. And the guys were trying to hang with T.I. and Jay-Z. I'd had lots of parties, but this sweet sixteen was the absolute best.

"This cake is off the charts," Diamond said as she came over and sat down between me and Troy.

"Isn't that like your third piece?" I asked.

"And?" She laughed. "Don't hate me because I'm

beautiful." She licked the frosting from the lemon crème cake from her lips.

I laughed, but it wasn't really a big fun laugh. What I really wanted was for Diamond to go away. There were a million other places where she could sit in this room. Why did she have to sit with me and Troy?

I mean, it wasn't like we had anything to hide. We were just chillin', talking about the contest. Talking about hanging out in Miami.

"So, when are we going to hang out?" he had asked me a few minutes ago.

I had said, "I guess soon," thinking that now I really did want to find out what Troy was all about. "Now that school is out, though I don't know if either one of us is gonna really have a lot of time. Sybil is going to rev up the rehearsals big time."

"Well then," Troy had said, getting a little closer to me, "we'll just have to do it in Miami. Let's just make a date now. Let's just say at some point, while we're in Florida, it's gonna be just you and me."

I hadn't had a chance to answer him because that's when Diamond had come over and plopped down in the middle of our conversation.

Just as I figured out a way to get rid of Diamond, I heard Stephen, a guy in my math class, yell out, "Get out! It's Zena!"

I almost broke my neck with how fast I turned my head. But that still wasn't as fast as Diamond; she jumped up and was gone in like two seconds flat!

This was just like Memorial Day—only this time, it was way worse. Now all my friends from school were going to wonder what Zena was doing here, and then they would find out that she was my mother.

I wasn't feelin' this.

While all the kids piled around Zena, Troy took my hand and squeezed it.

"I got you," he whispered.

But what could he do? Unless he knew of a way to wave his hand and make Zena disappear, I was stuck.

"Hello, everyone!" Zena laughed. She pushed her way through kids who were trying to get her autograph and taking pictures of her with their cell phones. But even though they crowded her, she still made her way to me.

Troy was still holding my hand when Zena came over and kissed my cheek.

"Happy birthday, sweetheart."

"Thanks," I said, praying this would be the end. I didn't want her to stay longer or create any more of a scene.

But I guess God didn't hear my prayer, because then Zena said, "I have a special gift for you."

My heart started doing that fast-beat thing again. "I don't want anything."

She held out her hand to me. "Come on. I think you'll like this."

I didn't want to go, but the way everybody was staring and whispering, I figured that the sooner I got this over with, the sooner we could just get back to my party.

I stood up, but left her hand hanging. I followed her, but the whole time I was wondering, Why is she doing this to me? What's going on?

She opened the front door, and there was this big scream. But it didn't come from me.

"Oh, my God!" Diamond screeched. "Look at that Range Rover!" My girl almost knocked me over to get through the door. But she wasn't the only one. It seemed that every kid that had been inside the house was outside now.

The only ones left inside were me and Troy. We were still in the doorway, because I couldn't move.

Zena didn't know it, though. She was all the way to the car before she realized that I wasn't hardly behind her.

When she looked back and saw me, she ran across the lawn and then tossed me the key. "Happy birthday! Something special for my sweet-sixteen girl."

"It's sweet, all right," Troy whispered before he let out a soft whistle. Like he was really impressed with Zena . . . and the truck.

While everybody was *ooh*ing and *aah*ing, I just looked at the shiny black Range Rover. Then at Zena. Then at the key. Back to Zena.

How embarrassing!

I handed her back the key. "No, thank you," I said, then turned around.

"Aaliyah!" she yelled after me.

But I was already gone. I ran down the hallway, straight to the bathroom. Went inside and locked the door.

In that tiny space, I walked back and forth and tried to figure out what had just happened. Why would Zena do that? Just walk into the middle of my party and give me a car?

Now all the kids were going to want to know what was up. And when they found out that she was my mother, the real questions would start. It would never be the same again.

Forget about all that forgiveness my dad was talking about—I was never going to forgive her for this.

I was huffin' and puffin' mad when someone knocked on the door.

I tried to put on my nice voice. "Just a minute," I said, like nothing was wrong. I wasn't sure if it was really someone who needed the bathroom or just someone trying to see what was going on with me.

Now I had to put on my nice face. And pretend like nothing had happened. Act like I didn't even know Zena.

I took a deep breath. But when I opened the door, all I wanted to do was cry.

Thank God the person who was standing on the other side of the door was my dad. And he was there to hold me.

Chapter 19

Ruining my life wasn't enough!

Zena just had to come to my birthday party and steal my shine, too. I couldn't believe it—how she had just walked in and tried to give me that key to a Range Rover. As if that was supposed to make me fall down at her feet. As if that would make her a good mother. As if that would make me want to be her daughter.

I rolled over on my bed and looked out the window. It was just getting dark outside. I wasn't even supposed to be home. Arjay had said that we were going to party all night for my birthday. Not that any of our parents were going to let us do anything all night long, but I wasn't supposed to be in my bedroom, lying in my bed at eight o'clock when the sun was just going down.

This was all Zena's fault.

After she came to the party, it didn't feel like fun anymore. It was the other kids who made it so bad for me. As soon as I came out of the bathroom, they were all over me, asking me all kinds of questions.

"Girl, is Zena really your mother?" "Girl, is that your new car?" "Girl, I thought your mother was dead!"

That was it—I couldn't take it anymore. So as fast as we could, India, Troy, and I gathered my presents and piled them into my dad's truck while Diamond just stood by the door watching us move back and forth and saying over and over to me, "Are you crazy?" every time I walked by.

Truth—I did feel kinda crazy. I mean, every kid I knew wanted a new car. And a Range Rover? That was off the chain. The thing is, if my dad had given me that car I would've been dancing on somebody's roof and outside right now driving all around Los Angeles. But it just didn't feel good coming from Zena.

"I wish you wouldn't leave, Pretty Lady," Troy had whispered to me right before I'd gotten into my dad's car.

"I gotta go," I told him. And then I promised that I would call him before our next rehearsal. But I felt bad when he said okay, 'cause I was pretty sure I was lying. My plan was to turn off my cell phone, because I knew it was going to be blowing up. Every kid at the party would be calling me, trying to find out the real deal. The only good thing about this was that school was out. I just hoped that by the time we went back in September, Zena would be long gone and totally forgotten.

I sighed. Hope. Hope. Hope. That's all I ever did when it came to Zena. I had hoped that she would go away. I had hoped that we would get a new mentor. I had hoped that I could drop out of the group. And now I was hoping that my business wouldn't be all over the streets. But none of the things I'd hoped and none of the prayers I'd prayed had been answered.

I rolled over again, not wanting to look out the window

anymore. It was horrible thinking about being home so early and by myself on my birthday.

Then I looked up, and shocker! Zena was standing in my doorway!

I just knew I had to be straight-up dreaming, because I hadn't heard the doorbell ring. And there was no way my dad would have ever let Zena come to my room. So I closed my eyes, said a quick prayer, and slowly opened them again.

And just like all the other times, my prayer wasn't answered, because she was still there.

I didn't take my eyes off her as I scooted up in my bed. Zena didn't move. Just stood there, looking all Hollywood in her denim pantsuit.

Finally, she said, "I'm sorry."

I didn't know what she wanted me to say, but I wasn't going to let her see me sweat. She'd already run me out of my party—that was all she was gonna get. "That's okay," I lied.

She shook her head and said, "I'm sorry."

Why did she say that again? I mean, I heard her the first time. "I just didn't want a car," I said, leaving out the part that I just didn't want a car *from her*.

She took little steps into my room, and then pointed to my bed like she wanted permission to sit down. Even though I just wanted to tell her to get out, I nodded, because like I said before, my dad had raised me right.

She looked around my bedroom. "This is nice," she said, looking at my bookcases, then at everything else. "I guess you like the color blue."

Duh? It didn't take a nuclear physicist to figure that out, since just about everything from the paint on the walls to my bedspread was blue.

"That's a nice new computer," she said when she looked at my desk.

Now I was ready to talk. I wanted her to know that I already had lots of nice things—without her. *"Dad* got me that for my birthday last year."

She was quiet; then she nodded and looked at me. "I'm sorry," she said again.

Okay, this was getting like totally redundant.

Then she explained, "And I'm not talking about the car."

Well, what was she talking about? I wanted to know, but I wasn't going to ask.

I didn't have to ask, because she told me, "When I was a little girl, I had big dreams."

This was not what I expected her to talk about, but I still kept my mouth shut.

She said, "But my biggest dream was to get married to a handsome, wonderful man and have a beautiful daughter."

Did she just say she wanted to have a daughter? Shocker! I didn't think she wanted any kids; I thought that was why she left.

She kept right on talking. "But the thing was, I had another dream. I wanted to be a singer." When she looked at me, she had tears in her eyes, and I don't know why, but I felt kinda sorry for her. "I am so sorry I left you."

I didn't mean to say anything, but I just had to ask her, "Then why did you?"

She shrugged a little. "I was young, and I didn't have my priorities straight. It was never my plan to leave and not come back. But then after your father and I talked, I started thinking that he was right—it wouldn't have been good for you if I came in and out of your life." She shook her head. "I really thought I was doing the right thing. I didn't think I could be a good mother because I had this thing inside of me"—she pressed her hands on her stomach, right where her diaphragm was—"that I couldn't get rid of." She stopped for a moment, like something surprised her. She was looking at my rocking chair.

"I can't believe you still have that." She walked over to the wooden chair and pushed it back and forth. "I used to rock you to sleep in this. Sing to you."

I said, "I remember that—a little."

When she looked at me, the tears were still in her eyes, but now the tears seemed to be in her smile, too. "Do you remember? Do you really?"

I shrugged. "I think so. Daddy told me that you used to make up songs with my name."

Her smile got a little bigger. "Heber remembers that? Yeah, I made up all kinds of songs." She sat back down on my bed. "I would sing, and you would coo like you were trying to sing with me." She laughed. "I knew then that you were going to be a great singer." Her smile went away. "Even back in those days, I used to imagine us on a stage together, singing. And all these years, I never gave up that thought or that dream. You and me together."

I couldn't believe she said that. "You thought about *me* while you were away?"

She looked at me with kind of a funny face. Like she was surprised that I had asked her that. "Every day! There wasn't a minute that went by when I didn't think about you, Aaliyah. You were never out of my heart, not one single day. I've loved you from the second I found out that I was pregnant until this very moment."

"But you never told anybody about me." I guess I had never said that aloud to anyone, but that was one thing that I'd been thinking. If Zena loved me, why did she keep me a secret? Why did she hide me away like she was ashamed of me? Why did she pretend that she didn't have a daughter?

"There were a few people who knew about you—like Josh."

I frowned; I didn't know who the heck Josh was.

"Josh, my manager," she said, like she knew what I was thinking. "I met Josh right here in L.A. when he was starting out, and I became his first big star." She stopped and let out a long breath. "It was partially his idea that I leave . . . not that I'm blaming him, because I was old enough to make my own decisions. But he thought it was best to create this whole persona, this whole glamorous woman, a sex symbol, he said." She laughed, like she didn't think she was any kind of sex symbol. When she stopped laughing, she said, "It was a mistake. It was all a mistake. And finally, I couldn't do it anymore." She looked at me, and the tears were back. "That's why I arranged to come home . . . this way. I thought it would be better. I thought it made sense."

"Wait a minute—you arranged this? I thought Glory 2 God called you."

She shook her head. "No, I arranged it. When I found out about you and the Divine Divas—"

"How? From Daddy?"

"No, I only spoke to your dad a few times over the years, but trust me, I had other ways to keep up with you." When she stopped, I could kinda tell that there was something she wanted to tell me. Then she said, "I've known a lot about you, sweetheart. I've kept up with how you were doing in school, who were your friends—I've known about your life."

Wow! I didn't know if that was scary or good. I mean, did she have cameras hidden in our house, in my room or something? I wanted to get up and check right now. But, I just sat there and listened some more.

"When I found out about the Divine Divas, I suggested this mentor program to Roberto."

"You know Mr. Roberto?" I asked. Not that I should've been surprised. According to Diamond—who was the expert on celebrities—all the famous people knew each other.

She nodded. "Yes, I've known Roberto for years, and he thought the mentor program was a great idea. I thought it was, too, but . . ." She stopped. "Roberto didn't know what I was doing, and I'm just sorry that I lied to everybody." She took another deep breath. "I can see now how this was more about me than you. I shouldn't have come back this way, but the truth is, I should've never left. And for that, you will never, ever know how sorry I am."

Okay, what was I supposed to say? That I forgave her? I mean, how could I? She had left me all by myself when I was just a little kid.

But I think she *was* waiting for me to forgive her, because when I didn't say anything, she made this little sound like she was trying to catch her breath. And then she leaned over, kissed my forehead, and stood up.

I knew I was supposed to say something, but I didn't have any words inside me. All I could do was watch her walk away.

And then Veronique came into my head. And her dad. And the funeral story. And for some reason, I didn't want Zena to leave.

Before she got to the door, I called her name.

She turned around.

I don't know why, but I said, "Thank you for the car."

She smiled like that was the best thing she'd ever heard.

And then I kept talking. "I have something for you, too."

She frowned, and my hands trembled as I went to my closet and pulled out the box. Inside, my head was telling me not to do this, not to show this to anyone, especially Zena, 'cause she was gonna think this was straight-up stupid. But inside where my heart was, I felt like Zena would want this, because no one had ever given her a Mother's Day card.

So I grabbed the box and sat down on the bed. When she sat next to me, I opened it for her. I showed her everything—the cards, the articles, even one letter that I had written to her on my thirteenth birthday.

For a long, long time, she didn't say a word. Just picked up every card slowly and read every word. I just watched her, and then I started to feel bad. She wasn't saying anything because she did think this was stupid.

All I wanted to do was grab the box from her and ask her to act like she'd never seen it. But then she looked at me and she was crying for real.

"I'm so sorry," she said again.

But this time, it was like I heard her.

"This . . . this . . ." She held up the first card that I had ever bought. "This is so beautiful."

She opened her arms, and it took me only a second to hug her back. I couldn't remember ever hugging my mother before, but the way she felt now—this was the best hug I had ever had.

Chapter 20

I couldn't say it was good, but it wasn't bad either.

I could say that it was weird, though—sitting at our table in the kitchen and eating pizza and cake with my dad and Zena. Yeah, it was straight-up weird, but I wasn't hatin' 'cause we were eating two of my fave foods in the world.

And this chocolate cake that Zena had ordered was ridiculous. Lots of frosting and crème. And it had taken her only like ten minutes to make a call and have it made for this party. Yup, a party—and it was all Zena's idea.

After we sat in my bedroom looking at the treasure chest, Zena said that she felt really bad that she had ruined my party. "So, let's have a party here," she said.

I didn't know what she meant until I came downstairs about a half an hour later and there she was in the kitchen with my dad and a big ole box of my favorite pizza. But what was even better was the cake. It tasted even better than it looked. I wanted to have another piece, but I had already had three and my stomach was beginning to hurt.

"So, a nuclear physicist?" Zena said to me.

This party was just my dad, Zena, and me, and we had been talking about lots of stuff. But it seemed that all Zena wanted to talk about was me.

I nodded and she said, "I don't even know what a nuclear physicist is . . . or does." She laughed.

People were always saying that to me. "It's just a form of physics," I said, like it was no big deal. "I wanna work for the government. I wish I was old enough now, 'cause if Barack Obama wins, I'd love to work for him."

"Wouldn't we all?" my dad said, and Zena laughed—well, she more like giggled.

I kinda frowned. What my dad said wasn't really funny, so why was she acting like it was?

"So you want to work for the president?" Zena asked after she stopped laughing. "I thought physicists worked in labs."

"Some do," I said. "But what I want to do is work for the State Department and study nuclear material."

"Wow," she said. Zena gave me one of those proud looks that my father always gave me.

I don't know why, but that made me feel kinda good this time. So, I kept on, "I really want to work on ways to use nuclear energy more effectively. I think in like twenty years, it's going to be an efficient source of energy for our country, and we really need it because we have to become less dependent on foreign countries for oil and other things."

Zena put down her fork and frowned. "Okay, there is no way that you're only sixteen."

"I am." I grinned. "Or I might do research so that we can better understand nuclear weapons." In a way, I felt like I was showing off. And truth—I was. But I really wanted Zena to know what I was all about. I wanted her to know that she didn't have a noob for a daughter.

She shook her head. "I knew you were smart, but some of that stuff you're talking about is way over my head."

My dad laughed and leaned back. Then, shocker—he put his arm around Zena's chair. Not like he was hugging her or anything, but it kinda made them look like a couple. Like his hand was supposed to be so close to her.

I didn't know what it was; the other day, I couldn't imagine them together. But today—well, they looked like they'd known each other for a long time.

Not that I wanted my dad to even think about Zena like that. Nuh-huh, not at all, no way, Jose.

I guess my father didn't notice the way I was staring at him because he kept right on talking. "Don't believe her, Aaliyah. None of that is going over her head. Your mother is really smart."

I smiled. Even though I still wasn't feelin' like Zena was my mother, hearing that didn't make me feel as bad as it did before.

My dad said, "Zena used to get all As, just like you."

"Really?" Now that surprised me, because I thought my dad was really smart, so I just thought that I got all of that from him. But Zena was smart, too?

"Yup," my dad said to me, then he turned to Zena. "If there're two things I remember about you, it's that you loved to read and loved to sing."

"I love to read," I said.

"I know." She winked at me and made me feel that proud thing again. "I have a collection of books that I want to give to you. A lot of first editions."

First a car, and now books. "Really?" I had never been into collecting books, but India and I had gone to a book signing for Maya Angelou, one of my favorite authors, and I was thinking that maybe I should start collecting. Maybe now I would. "Okay, thanks."

She looked down at her watch. "I cannot believe that it's almost midnight." Smiling, she looked at me and said, "Your birthday is almost over. Anyway, I'd better get out of here." She stood and started picking up our plates.

"No," my dad said. "I'll clean up."

She looked at him like he was crazy. "You? I thought you hated this kind of stuff."

"I did, but I had to—" And then, he stopped. They stared at each other; both of them looked kinda sad.

Now what was I supposed to do? I mean, should I stay, should I help? I wasn't sure, so I took the easy way out.

"I'm gonna go to bed." And then it got worse, because I *really* didn't know what to do now. Was I just supposed to say good night? Or was I supposed to say good night and hug Zena? Did she think I was gonna kiss her? Not!

But it seemed like Zena didn't have any questions. She just walked over to me as if she'd been saying good night to me forever. Standing real close, she said, "You don't know how much this meant to me. To share your birthday with you." Then she hugged me, and you know what? That felt exactly like what she was supposed to do. "I'll see you at rehearsal on Monday, okay?"

I nodded, then looked at my father, who was smiling. But he had kind of a sad look in his eyes. I hoped he didn't think I was liking Zena more than I loved him. I said, "Daddy, do you want me to help you clean up?"

He shook his head. "Go on up and get some rest. You've had a long day."

"Okay." I kissed his cheek, then turned around real fast and ran up the stairs.

Inside my bedroom, the first thing I saw was the treasure chest still on my bed. Without even thinking about it, I picked up the box and took it downstairs.

"Zena," I said. She was standing at the counter, wrapping up what was left of the cake. I took a deep breath and said, "I want you to have this."

The tears came right to her eyes, and I hoped she wasn't going to do that crying thing again. But she didn't go all the way. She put down the plastic wrap she was holding and came over to me.

"Thank you," was all she said as she took the box.

My dad was frowning like he was wondering what was going on, but I knew that Zena would explain it to him. I just hoped he didn't think that I was a dumb little kid for saving all of that stuff.

But as I went back upstairs, I had a feeling that my dad wasn't going to think that. And by the time I got back up to my bedroom, I was feeling really good. I was feeling like today had been a good day. And like tonight it was going to be really easy to close my eyes and go to sleep.

Chapter 21

I knew this was going to be a shocker for my girls.

No way did they think I would be driving to rehearsal in my new SUV. Last thing they knew, I had turned Zena down cold. And yesterday at church, I'd let them keep thinking that. None of them had said a single word to me about my party or my Range Rover. It was like they'd been scared that if they'd said anything, I would have cried or something. Even Diamond had been supernice—well, as nice as she could be, because the world was really still just about her.

But I'd let them think what they wanted to think. Even when we'd hung out after church, I'd just thanked them for the spa day and hadn't even mentioned the party.

But today, my dad gave me the lecture on all the driving rules, and he checked out the car himself. He set up my cell phone on the Bluetooth so that I would never have to hold my phone while I was in the car, he gave me lessons on how to use the nav system, told me that he was going to pay the insurance but that I had to take care of my own gas, and then he made me drive around with him for like an hour before he said I was ready to roll.

On the whole ride over here, I couldn't believe how excited I was. I wasn't sure if I was excited because I finally had my own hot car or because I knew my girls were gonna freak when they saw me.

That's what I was thinking when I rolled up behind Diamond in Hope Chapel's parking lot. Her visor was down, and as usual she was checking herself out in the mirror. At first she looked behind her like she was wondering who was rocking a Range Rover.

But then she recognized me. And her eyes got big. And she scooted out of her car. And starting screaming like she was a crazy person.

The way she was jumping up and down, I thought she might have one of her fake heart attacks for real.

"You kept the car!"

My windows were rolled up, but I heard her yelling the same thing over and over.

I parked and got out of the car slowly, as if my driving a brand-new, shiny black Range Rover was no big deal.

"You kept the car!" she screamed as if she thought this was the first time I would hear her.

"Yeah, you said that already." I was trying to keep a straight face, like I was all nonchalant and everything, but that only lasted a second. I started grinning just like Diamond.

"I thought you had given it back to Zena," Diamond started blubbering. "I mean, I thought that was the dumbest thing in the world, but I was like, hey, if she wants to be dumb, let her be dumb. I mean, I would never be that dumb myself, but I was gonna let you just roll the way you roll 'cause you know how you are. You never—"

"Would you just be quiet!" I said like I was mad, but we both knew I wasn't.

Diamond grinned and hugged me. "Happy birthday, girl. Welcome to the wonderful world of being grown and known."

We walked into the church together, but Diamond didn't give me a chance to tell my own news.

"She kept the car," she yelled out before I had a chance to say anything. And then she started jumping up and down again like the Range Rover belonged to her.

"I'm glad you did, my sistah." Veronique hugged me. I could tell she was happy for me, but she wasn't acting like a nutcase like Diamond.

India just grinned. "I knew you would." And then she started talking about some jewelry she saw in a magazine that she was going to try to make. See, that's why I loved my BFFL. She knew when to make something a big deal and when to just let something ride. 'Cause truth—I was tired of me and Zena being a big deal to everybody. I just wanted us to be normal—or at least as normal as we could be.

"Where're the guys?" I asked, dropping my bag on the floor. I couldn't wait to tell Troy that I had kept the car.

"The guys?" Diamond asked. "Or do you mean Troy?" She giggled like we were in the third grade or something.

"I mean what I said—where're the *guys?*"

India said, "Sybil told us Zena just wanted to rehearse with us tonight since we're going to be practicing that second song. They're not going to be dancing on that one."

I nodded, but I was kinda disappointed. I hadn't spoken to Troy since my birthday, and I knew I should've given him a call. I'm not sure why I hadn't; I liked hanging out with him, but I just felt better being with him when there were other people around.

"Hello, ladies."

I turned around and felt myself break into a big ole smile when Zena and Sybil walked into the room. That kinda shocked me—I was acting like I was glad to see Zena. But hey, how could I hate? It turned out that I had a birthday that was off the charts because of her.

Diamond said, "She kept the car!" as if Zena didn't know. Or maybe she was saying it to Sybil—I couldn't tell.

But it didn't seem to matter to Zena or Sybil, because all they did was smile.

Zena dropped her bag on the floor and said, "I want to get right to work because we don't have that much time left to get this song right." She stopped and looked at us. "I'm excited about working on our duets, and I hope you are, too."

She was looking at me, but Diamond said, "Are you kidding me? I'm going to be singing with Zena. I am more than excited." She started waving her hand in her face, like she needed air. Like she was going to faint.

Zena frowned, but India, Veronique, and I all rolled our eyes.

"Are you okay?" Zena asked Diamond.

Sybil didn't even give Diamond a chance to answer. "She's fine," she said to Zena as she handed out the sheet music for the song that we were going to sing. "Diamond is our drama queen. She always acts like this."

"Oh," Zena said, like it seemed crazy to her. But that seemed to be her clue to keep right on moving, because all she said after that was, "Let's get started." She looked down at the music in her hand. "I'm so glad that you all agreed to sing this. It's one of my favorite songs."

"It was easy for us to choose," India said, "since Jackie wrote it."

We all nodded. Glory 2 God had given us a list of songs for the duets with our mentor, and we'd all gone ballistic when we'd seen "My Help," by Jackie Gouche, on the list. Jackie was our minister of music at Hope Chapel and the head of all the church choirs.

And her song "My Help" was off the chain. People all over the country were singing it. I'd heard it at other church services, at my cousin's wedding in Maryland and even at my Uncle Ray's funeral. But now we were going to get to sing it in this big contest. Maybe Jackie would become really famous—like Zena—after this.

Zena sat down on the tall stool on the side of the piano. "Now the way this part is going to work," she explained, "is I have to sing the first stanza and then you each join in with me for one part before we all sing together. So, how should we do this? Who goes first?"

For the first time since Zena had been working with us, I raised my hand without waiting for one of my girls to answer. "We should do it in order," I said, like I was in charge. "You sing," I said, pointing to Zena. "Then, Diamond, India, Veronique . . ." I paused, because I knew this was going to be the part that Zena liked best. "And you and I will sing together last."

I was just giving the order of the song, but the way it got quiet and the way they were all staring at me, you would've thought I had walked right up to Zena and kissed her or something.

Zena took a deep breath, then looked at my girls. "What do you think of that?"

Like she had to ask. My girls always went along with what I said; I was the mature one, so they always followed.

Don't hate!

Just like I thought, my girls nodded. Diamond looked down at the music that Sybil had given us and said, "We don't need this; we know the words by heart."

"Then let's get to singing," Zena said. "We'll sing it straight the first time and see if there's anything we need to change."

Sybil sat down at the piano, but then she stood up real slow and said, "I have a surprise for you." She grinned, then held out her arm to the door, like she was presenting someone famous to us.

Since Zena was already in the room, I wasn't worried about who else might be coming in. The door opened slowly, and we all cheered when Jackie walked in. We ran over to her, and she hugged all of us.

"I couldn't believe that you girls chose my song," she said, like she was so surprised.

"Why wouldn't we?" Veronique said. "It's just one of the best gospel songs ever written!"

"Ever!" Diamond, India, and I said together.

Zena laughed. "Well, the Divine Divas have spoken, Jackie, and I agree with them." She turned to us. "That's why I asked Jackie to play. We won't be using a track in Miami. We're going with the real deal. Jackie will be onstage, live, with us."

"Get out!" Diamond shouted, and we cheered again.

But this play time didn't last long. All of a sudden, Zena, Sybil, and Jackie got real serious.

"Let's get started, Divas!" Jackie sat down at the piano, and we all stood behind Zena, who stayed on the stool.

When Jackie hit that first note and Zena sang, "I will lift up my eyes to the hills. . . ." chills ran through my body. I just loved this song, and I didn't think that anyone could rock it like Jackie, but the way Zena sounded made me want to cry. And we weren't even on a stage yet. How would she sound when we had the right microphones and everything?

Then it was Diamond's turn to join Zena. Diamond sang, "He said He would not suffer thy foot, thy foot to be moved. The Lord that keepeth thee . . ."

I didn't know what it was, but Diamond had never sounded better.

Then, Zena and India, "Oh, the Lord is thy keeper, the Lord is thy shade, upon thy right hand . . ."

Whoa! Was that India? Check her out. My girl always said that she was the worst singer of all of us, but not today!

Veronique sang, "No, the sun shall not smite thee by day, nor the moon by night. . . ."

I knew Vee was going to bring it—and she did. Okay, that just meant that I had to do my thing.

I took a deep breath, looked at Zena, and sang, "My help!" I kept my eyes on Zena and tried to remember all the things she'd taught us about singing from our center and singing with our heart. "My help! My help! All of my help cometh from the Lord!" I held that last note until I thought I was gonna faint.

Whew! I thought. Okay, now I was ready to hit the chorus with Zena and my girls. But something happened—everybody stopped singing. I looked around.

"What's wrong?"

My girls were staring at me like they had never seen me before. Even Zena, Sybil, and Jackie had stopped.

"What's wrong?" I asked again.

Veronique stepped to me. "My sistah, I ain't never heard you sing like that. You sound just like . . ." She stopped and looked at Zena. Behind Veronique, Diamond and India were nodding their heads, looking all serious, like they were going to cry.

And then I looked at Zena, and she was crying. But she didn't say anything—all she did was hug me.

"Okay," she said after she pulled away from me. Jackie handed Zena a tissue and said, "Let's take it from the top and see if we can get through the whole song without any tears, all right?"

Sybil said, "That's gonna be hard the way you girls sound." She shook her head. "I cannot wait to get to Miami."

I didn't know what the big deal was. I mean, yeah, I knew I sounded good, but we all did. I figured it was because of Zena. Singing with her just made me want to be better, and I was sure that's what happened with Diamond, India, and Veronique, too.

Jackie started playing again and my girls and I all got ready for our parts. I hoped Zena wasn't going to cry again. I mean, she was going to have to work that out—she didn't want to break down like this in Miami.

But I guess I couldn't hate—she had told me that this had always been her dream. To sing with me. I wanted to tell her that it was cool for me, too, but I decided I'd wait until after the contest. Because if I told her that now, she might never, ever stop crying.

Chapter 22

I felt like I had a job!

Straight-up—the way we had been practicing every day for the past two weeks, I felt like somebody needed to give me a paycheck. But it was fun—now that I kinda liked Zena. And it was even better when the guys were at rehearsals with us. While we spent every other day working with Zena on our duets, the guys were working with Turquoise—for all the hours we had been singing, they had been dancing. And it showed when they put their moves together with our singing. The Divine Divas and the Three Ys Men were poppin'! To me, we looked even better than we had at the semifinals in New York.

Troy was the best dancer, of course, and I wasn't just saying that because I liked him. It was just the way he moved. He could bend and twist his body all kinds of ways, like he was a pretzel or something. Anyway, he could hold it down.

But right about now, I didn't want to think about dancing or singing or nothing. My big Saturday plan was to spend the whole morning in bed, because I was tired.

145

I was so glad that Zena was giving us this whole weekend off. It had to be her idea, because Sybil had never given us this much time right before the contest. Sybil worked us until the last day, the last hour, the last minute.

But even though we were leaving for Miami in just three days, Zena said that the most important part of any performance was knowing when to rest. That didn't make a lot of sense to me, 'cause I would think we should be practicing until the last minute. But since Zena was the one with all of the Grammys, I kinda figured that she knew a little something.

Whether Zena was right or wrong, I didn't really care. All I knew was that my bed felt real good and I was gonna catch up on some Saturday morning TV. Just as I grabbed my remote, my cell phone rang.

Dang! I didn't really want to talk to anyone, but then I started thinking that it might be my BFFL. I grabbed my cell and frowned when I saw the number. But I clicked on the Talk button anyway.

"Hi, Zena," I said, surprised that she wasn't calling on our home phone like she always did.

"Good morning. I was hoping to catch you before you went out. Are you busy?"

"No, I'm cool. What's up?"

"Well, I wanted to know if you would join me this morning for breakfast—or brunch, actually, because as long as it takes for me to get ready, it will be closer to noon." She laughed.

"Oh, sorry. But Daddy had to work today. He didn't tell you?"

"No," she said. "But I wasn't calling for him. This invitation is for you . . . to have brunch with me."

That made me sit up straight in my bed. No wonder she hadn't called on our house phone. Zena wanted me to go out with her—just the two of us.

Nuh-huh. I mean, we were starting to be cool and every-thing, but that's because we were always around other people. We'd eaten a lot together, but my dad had always been there. Or we'd been at rehearsal and Sybil would run out and get us sandwiches. But being somewhere when it was just the two of us—no! I wasn't ready for that.

"Aaliyah?" Zena called my name when I didn't say any-thing. "You don't have any other plans, do you?"

I wanted to lie so bad, but I couldn't think of a good lie to tell. So, I told the truth. "No," I mumbled, and then I wanted to kick myself. Why couldn't I be a better liar?

"Great. Let's meet at the Beverly Hills Hotel. They have the best weekend brunch. I'll call over and make reservations. What time can you be ready?"

See, if she hadn't bought me that car, I would've had a good excuse. I would've been able to say that I didn't have a ride—though that wouldn't have worked anyway. She would've just come over here in her big ole limousine.

"Uh . . . I don't know." I was stalling, trying to come up with something.

Zena said, "Well, let's just say we'll meet at noon. That'll give me almost three hours. Is that good for you?"

I told her yes because I didn't have anything else to say. And when I hung up, I jumped out of bed.

I didn't want to have brunch or anything with Zena by my-self. What were we going to talk about? What was I going to say?

"Okay," I said as I walked back and forth in my room. I was the smart one, the mature one—I could figure this out.

That's when I came up with the perfect solution. My girls. I would take one of them with me.

India would've been my first choice, but with Zena, Diamond was better. I loved my girl, but Diamond wasn't nothin' but a Zena groupie. And if she could have brunch with just Zena, me, and her, she would talk the whole time. She would talk so much that Zena wouldn't even remember that I was there.

I'm brilliant! I thought while I dialed Diamond's number. But when Diamond's phone went straight to voice mail, I hung up and tried it again. And again. But all I kept getting was her voice mail.

What's up with that? It was way too early for her to be at the mall.

I started thinking about my BFFL again, but the thing was, India was just too quiet. If it was me and India, Zena would be all over me. Veronique would be better—not as good as Diamond, but definitely better than India.

I was so glad when she answered on the first ring that I didn't know what to do. I started talking fast. "Vee, I need a huge solid," I said right after I said hello.

"You know how we roll, my sistah. Anything."

"Great. I'll be there to pick you up; you're going to brunch with me and Zena."

"I can't. I'm watching my brothers."

Dang! That was the story of Veronique's life. She always had to babysit her brothers on the weekend.

"But I need you!" I whined like a baby.

"Okay, this must be really bad, 'cause you're sounding like Diamond. What's up?"

"I don't want to have brunch with Zena all by myself."

"Why not?" Veronique asked, as if what I just said didn't make any sense. "She's your mom—you can eat with her."

The thing was, that's what they all thought. They thought that since Zena was my mother, and since she'd bought me that car, and since I had stayed in the Divine Divas, that everything was all right now.

It wasn't that easy for me, though. I mean, I was cool with Zena, but there were times when I still felt funny around her. It was because there were these little thoughts in my head that still made me mad, that made it hard for me to forget that she'd left me and hard to let her just come back now like everything was all right.

All of that stuff in my head made it hard for me to want to connect with Zena all the way.

"Well, anyway," Veronique continued, "I can't go. What about Diamond . . . oh, wait, she and India are with The Judge and Drama Mama picking up our outfits," she said, calling Ms. Elizabeth and Ms. Tova by the names that Diamond had made up for them.

"That's right," I said, feeling like I was in big trouble now. I'd totally forgotten about that.

"Hey, I got an idea!" Veronique was so excited, I felt better already. She said, "Call Troy!"

The little bit of excitement I felt went away. "Troy?" I asked, like I had never heard his name before.

"Yeah, he's been trying to get you to go out with him. He'd be perfect."

I wasn't sure about that, but by the time I hung up with Veronique, I decided that Troy was good—especially since I didn't have anyone else.

So I took a deep breath and dialed his number. Even though I was nervous, I smiled when he answered the phone. "Hey, Pretty Lady!"

"How did you know it was me?" I asked as I sat back down on my bed.

"How do you think? Your number's programmed into my cell. I've been just waiting for you to break down and finally call me." He laughed. "I knew it. I knew you were into me."

For the first time since Zena called, I laughed. That was

one thing I really liked about Troy—he always made me laugh.

"So, what's up?" he asked.

I closed my eyes and said, "Well, I was wondering if you wanted to go out and have brunch—at the Beverly Hills Hotel."

"Whoa, you wanna roll like that? Well, I don't know if I got Beverly Hills money."

"That's okay."

"No, it's not," he said, sounding really serious now. "I pays for mine, and I'm not taking you out and letting you pay for anything. Let's just start with a movie. I can spring for that and some popcorn and soda."

Okay, I was gonna have to come correct and tell the truth. I just prayed he wouldn't say no.

"Well, it's not exactly brunch with just me." I took a deep breath. "Zena wants me to go to brunch with her and I want you to go with me." I said the words so fast that the whole sentence sounded like one word.

When he was quiet for so long, I wasn't sure that he had heard me. "Troy?"

"Yeah, I'm here." And then he said, "You just want me to go because you don't want to be alone with her, huh?"

I was busted. He was right and I was wrong for trying to use him like this.

But before I could apologize, he said, "Sure, I'll go. I told you before, I got you, Pretty Lady. I got you."

I didn't know if I should jump up and down or cry. "Thank you, Troy. Thank you."

"No prob. One thing, though, I'm not driving. I'm not rollin' like you."

"That's okay. I can pick you up—you okay with that?" I asked thinking about what he'd just said about paying for everything himself.

"Yeah, I'll give you a couple of dollars for gas."

I was about to tell him no, but I kinda liked that he wanted to pay for everything. My dad had told me that that's how guys should be.

We made plans to meet at eleven thirty and I thanked him again before I hung up.

Okay, I'd done it, but it was still gonna be weird. I liked Zena and I liked Troy. But for some reason, I didn't want to be out with either of them alone. Well, I wouldn't be alone—it would be the three of us.

This was going to be straight-up interesting.

Chapter 23

Troy really was kinda hot!

That's what I was thinking as he did that bad-boy strut out of his house. I liked his style—he was wearing black jeans and a tight black T-shirt. He kinda matched the black pants and black baby tee I was wearing. We were kinda dressed like a couple.

"Yo, what's up, Pretty Lady?" he said as he jumped into my car.

"Nothing. Thanks again for doing this for me."

He nodded his head and just stared, like he was trying to look right through me. I was glad that I was driving, so that I could act like I was focusing on the road. It was really quiet, but I couldn't think of anything to say.

Maybe this was why I hadn't wanted to go out with Troy before. I mean, when I was with my girls, it was easy—we just talked about whatever came in our heads. And sometimes, it was even easy to talk to some of the guys at school—especially the ones who loved science class or hung out in the library. But most of the time, kids bored me—and with the things I liked to talk about, I bored them, too.

The longer we drove without talking, the quieter it got. I wanted to turn on the radio and put it on blast, but that would've been rude. I had to think of something—come up with anything—to say.

"So, what were you doing this morning?" I asked. And then I thought, *Lame, lame, lame!* Couldn't I have come up with something better than that? I should've talked to Diamond about this; she would've given me the four-one-one on how to act and what to say to guys.

But my question didn't seem to bother Troy, because he said, "I was watching this cool documentary on Richard Wright."

"Really?" I said. My mouth was opened so wide. "I love him—he's one of my favorite writers."

"Stop playin'." He leaned back in his seat like he was trying to get a better look at me. "I've read all his books—twice!"

I looked at Troy sideways; why didn't I know this about him before? He didn't look like much of a reader to me, though I really couldn't tell you what a reader looked like. I said, "You're the one who needs to stop playin'. Okay, what's your favorite Richard Wright book?"

He stayed quiet for so long that I started to feel bad. I knew he was playin'; he probably hadn't read any of Richard Wright's books. He probably hadn't even heard of him before this morning. He probably didn't even like to read. Why'd he have to do that just when I was beginning to really like him?

Then he said, "It's hard for me to decide—I really liked *Native Son* 'cause I was feelin' Bigger Thomas and all that he had to go through. But then, I was diggin' *Black Boy* because a lot of people don't know, but that was Wright's true-to-life story."

Wow! He *had* read Richard Wright, and he was takin' it deep.

"Those are my favorites, but I loved his short stories in *Uncle Tom's Children,* too."

"They were all right." Troy shook his head. "But when I read, I want the *whole* story. I don't like nothin' short."

I laughed. "So you like to read? I've never seen you with anything but a textbook."

"I've never seen you with anything but a textbook either. What does that mean?"

Okay, now see—I was feelin' Troy. 'Cause he just straight-up told it—just like me. I asked, "Have you read Claude Brown's book?"

Now it was Troy who looked at me sideways. "Girl, what you know about Claude Brown? He was my uncle."

"Get out!" I said, "Claude Brown, the author, was *your* uncle?"

He laughed. "Nah, I'm just playin', but I loved his book *Manchild in the Promised Land* so much, I *wish* he was my uncle. Man, I wish I'd met him before he died."

"Yeah, that would've been cool. I met Maya Angelou a couple of months ago."

"Stop playin'!"

After that, we didn't need any kind of music or anything in the car. We had each other, and we talked all the way to Beverly Hills. And the whole time we were riding, I was thinking that I should've gone out with Troy a long time ago.

As soon as I turned in front of the Beverly Hills Hotel, all the good feelings I had riding over with Troy went straight out the window. When I stopped in front of the valet, I saw Zena standing right in the front of the lobby. I couldn't tell if she saw me or not 'cause she didn't move.

I kept my eyes on her as we waited for the attendant. She didn't look anything like herself today. Whenever she came to my house or to rehearsals, she was always so sharp, like a diva, lookin' Hollywood. Her hair was always tight, with long curls flowing down her back, and her clothes were always covered in rhinestones or fur or some other expensive stuff.

But today Zena just looked like everybody else hanging out in Beverly Hills. Her hair was tucked under an Obama baseball cap and she had on sunglasses so dark you couldn't see her eyes and so wide you could hardly see her face.

When the parking attendant came over, I slid out of the front seat slowly, handed him my keys, then walked toward Zena. She smiled when she saw me, but then her face changed when she saw Troy. Her smile turned upside down just a little.

"Hi, sweetheart," she said, hugging me.

I gave her two little taps on her back like I always did. She always hugged me, but it was hard for me to really hug her back.

Then she turned to Troy, and her smile was right back on her face. "Troy, how are you?" She hugged him, too.

"Great, Ms. Z."

"Well," she said, "let's go in." She walked ahead of us for a couple of steps and then, over her shoulder, she said, "I only made reservations for two."

Uh-oh. Maybe I shouldn't have done it exactly like this. But I really hoped she could get Troy in with us, since I was having such a good time with him. And what was the big deal anyway? This was only a restaurant.

Troy said, "I'm sorry, Ms. Z, but I called Aaliyah this morning, and when she said she was gonna hang out with you, I just bogarted. Hope it's not going to be a problem."

I opened my mouth wide when Troy told that lie.

Zena said, "Don't worry; it's no problem." She smiled again. "I'm glad you could join us."

When Zena went to talk to the hostess, I whispered to Troy, "You didn't have to lie like that."

He whispered back, "No worries. I told you, I got you. Always."

Before I could say anything else, Zena came back, and the three of us followed the hostess. As we were passing through the crowded tables, those big glasses that Zena had on weren't doing a good job of hiding her, 'cause lots of people were looking and pointing. I was surprised that I felt kinda proud—and then I thought about it. None of those people knew who I was; they would never know. There was nothing for me to feel proud about.

The hostess stopped at a table, waited until we all sat down, and then handed us menus.

But before I could get mine opened, Troy asked the lady, "Where's the restroom?"

"I'll be right back," he said after the hostess told him to follow her.

I could not believe that Troy had just gone and left me like that. He could have waited at least a minute before he left me alone with Zena.

I opened my menu and read real slow. All I could do was hope that Troy would get back here fast, 'cause I could feel Zena staring at me.

"I'm glad you brought Troy with you," she said, putting down her menu. "He seems like a nice young man."

I couldn't be rude, so I put my menu down, too. "Troy's cool, but we're only friends." I wanted to make it clear.

"Of course. What else would you be at sixteen?" she answered in a tone that sounded like she was my mother.

Then her smile went away. "You didn't want to do this, did you?"

I knew what she was talking about, but I still said, "What?"

"Have lunch. You didn't want to do this with me."

"Yeah, I did." I tried to make that sound like the truth, but the way she shook her head let me know that she knew I was lying.

"You're afraid to be alone with me," she said.

How did she know? And then I thought about what Diamond always said—that if you weren't careful, mothers could figure out everything. Diamond said you had to stay one step ahead if you wanted to outsmart them because mothers were definitely smarter than fathers.

Just a little while ago, I had wished that I'd talked to Diamond about Troy. Now I wished that I'd talked to her about Zena.

I still didn't have an answer for Zena, but it didn't matter because she said, "I can understand you not being comfortable around me yet."

"You do?" For the first time since I sat down, I felt like I could breathe.

She nodded. "This is still hard for you. It's easier for me because being with you is what I've always wanted. But this is not what you've always wanted."

"No, it is," I said. "I always wanted you to be here, living in L.A. with me. I just never thought . . ." I stopped.

She nodded, like she understood the words I didn't even say. After a while, she said, "I told you before that I was sorry."

Now I felt bad. Did she think I wanted her to beg or something? "I'm not asking you to say that again."

"I know you're not. But what I'm talking about is not you. It's me . . . and what I've said. I told you that I was sorry, but I never asked for your forgiveness."

Why would she ask me for that? I mean, yeah, I was sixteen. But compared to her, I was just a kid. Why would she ask *me* for forgiveness?

She said, "I've asked God to forgive me for making terrible choices." She reached over and put her hand over mine. "But I didn't ask you." Looking straight into my eyes, she said, "Aaliyah, sweetheart, can you forgive me, please?"

My lips started trembling, and I prayed to God that I wouldn't start crying in this fancy restaurant. I didn't really know what she meant. What was I supposed to do? How would I really know if I had forgiven her?

It took me a while, but I finally told her the truth. "I don't know how to do that," I whispered. " 'Cause I still have a lot of little mad thoughts in my head. I keep thinking about all the times when you weren't here and I felt so bad. I think about . . ." I just couldn't say any more.

Now Zena had tears in her eyes, too. It would be worse if she started crying, because people already knew who she was and then everybody would be talking about how the famous Zena was crying inside the Beverly Hills Hotel.

She squeezed my hand. "I think the only way you're going to be able to forgive me is if God helps you. True forgiveness can only come with His help."

"Really?"

She nodded. "Forgiving is one of the hardest things to do. For some reason, it's easier for people to hold onto bad feelings than try to find good feelings. But God knows that. And that's why He tells us that He wants us to forgive and that He will help us."

"I want . . . I want to forgive you. I just don't . . ."

The way her face was all scrunched up now, I knew she was gonna cry for sure. She said, "Well then, let's pray."

"Here?" I looked around. No, she didn't want me to bow

my head and pray right now—not while all of these people were around us. And what about Troy? He was going to be back any minute, and he would think we were crazy if he saw us sitting here praying like we were in church or something.

But Zena nodded—like she really expected me to bow my head. "I would love to pray with you." It must've been the way I was looking at her that made her say, "Don't be scared, I'll pray."

"But what about—"

"The people? I don't care about them," she said all calmly, as if praying in the middle of a restaurant was no big thing. "I only care about you . . . and God. And I have a feeling that He doesn't care where we pray."

I was trying, trying to figure out a way to get out of this. But it didn't seem like Zena was gonna let me. She didn't even wait for me to say yes; she just bowed her head. I didn't have a choice—I did the same thing.

She prayed, thanking God for bringing me back into her life. And she thanked Him for understanding and forgiving all the things she'd done wrong. Then she asked God to help me forgive her the way He had forgiven her.

That part made me feel bad, because when I was little, in Sunday school we had to memorize that scripture about how we all fall short. Comparing me to God? Talk about fallin' short!

And then, shocker—she asked God to move my heart so that I could not only forgive her but love her, too.

It was a good thing my head was bowed because I don't know what kind of look I had on my face. I mean, I liked Zena now—but love her?

Even though my head was down, I kept peeking, with one eye, checking to see if anyone was watching us. And I was definitely trying to peep to see if Troy was coming back. I wanted to see him before he saw us.

When she said, "Amen," I was glad to lift my head.

But then something really weird happened.

I looked at Zena. And it was like those tiny mad thoughts that were in my head slowly went away. Because all I could think about was Veronique. And her dad. And truth—I was really glad that Zena had come back now and not later . . . when it was too late.

Just thinking about that made me stand up a little, and before I knew it, I reached across the table. For the first time ever, I hugged Zena before she hugged me. Just as I did that, Troy came back.

"Okay, I'm ready." He grinned as he sat down. "Did I miss anything?"

Zena looked at me. I looked at her. We both looked at Troy. And then Zena and I busted out laughing.

Chapter 24

According to Diamond, who knew all things about every-thing, we were on the Rodeo Drive of South Beach. If I had known that this was where we were coming, I might have stayed at the hotel with the guys. Not that I was trying to just hang out with Troy; it was all this shopping that Diamond had us doing. We walked up and down Lincoln Road, going into every single one of the little shops. At first, it was kind of fun, but now I was ready to go, because shopping really wasn't my thing.

But it wasn't just Diamond who was acting like a serial shopper. Her mom, Ms. Elizabeth, was puttin' a hurtin' on her credit cards, too. And Ms. Tova and India were doing the same thing. Even Veronique and her mom. Ms. Lena *never* came to any of our competitions. So when I saw her on the plane yesterday, I almost fell over. And now, here she was in Florida, hanging out with us and shopping like she'd just won the lottery.

And then there was Zena.

Now, she took shopping to a whole 'nother level, because her limo driver came with us. Even though we were walking, Mr. James drove down every street we walked. And whenever we came out of one store, he was right there, piling our bags into the limousine so that we didn't have to carry a thing.

In the beginning, it was fun. I mean, Diamond, India, and Veronique were my girls for a lot of years, but never before had we all hung out with our mothers. It was straight-up weird, but fun.

And it was kinda fun whenever anyone recognized Zena 'cause her fans went crazy. Even though she had on a hat and those huge sunglasses again, it was hard for her to walk one block without someone screaming her name. She had signed so many autographs, her hand had to be hurting. And whenever anyone stopped Zena, Diamond jumped right in and told them about the Divine Divas.

Now, that was just hilarious—especially with the way some people looked at Diamond like *who are you?*

But the fun was starting to slip away, because I could never hang at shopping the way my girls could. Not only that, nobody seemed to notice that we hadn't eaten a thing since this morning. Somebody needed to feed me before I passed out.

"Okay, this is the last store," I said. I didn't think any of them were listening to me, but I meant it. If they went into another store, I was gonna call my dad and tell him that these people were starving me. He'd come get me for sure.

But then, food left my mind when I bumped into this table that had a stack of white jeans. I picked up a pair and almost lost my mind—they were tight! White denim, with rhinestone down the sides and on the pockets and the belt loops. And two rhinestone hearts on the butt.

"These are fierce," Diamond said, picking up a pair of her own. "I love these! I'm gonna get them, are you?"

"Definitely," I said. It didn't matter to me that we had the same clothes—we had all been shopping together since we were little; we had a lot of the same things.

I held the jeans up in front of me and kinda modeled in the mirror. Oh yeah, I could see myself in them—maybe even on that first date that Troy kept talking about, because he said that he didn't count going out to brunch with Zena any kind of date.

"Those are cute," India said. "But I can't wear white."

"Why not?"

"Have you seen my booty? Please." Then, with the way I looked at her, she said, "Don't worry; I like the way I look, I just know not to put my butt in white pants."

I was laughing when Zena came over to me.

"I love those jeans," she said.

I grinned. "So do I." Then I looked at the price tag. Were they kidding me? Two hundred and forty dollars? That would fill my gas tank for six months! I put the jeans right back on the table.

Zena asked, "What's wrong?" as she grabbed the pants and looked them over herself.

I shook my head. "They cost too much." I was ready to move on to the T-shirts.

"Oh, don't worry about that; I'll get them for you."

"No," I told her, as if I was the mother. "They're too expensive."

She was smiling when she leaned close to me and whispered, "I have a secret. I can afford it."

She may have thought that was funny, but for some reason I didn't. Truth—what she said made me feel kinda bad.

I took the jeans out of her hand. "That's okay, I'll find something else. And I have my own money."

Her face looked like I had hurt her feelings, but that's not what I wanted to do. I mean, I knew she had the money—she didn't have to tell me that. I just didn't want her to think that I thought of her like that. Like she was just an ATM. I didn't want her to think that all I wanted was her money.

And like I told her, I had my own. My dad had given me plenty to shop with . . . I just didn't want to spend it all on one pair of jeans.

Slowly, Zena walked away, and India came up behind me. "What's up with that?" my BFFL asked. "Why wouldn't you let her buy them for you?"

For all the years that India and I had been best friends, I couldn't remember a time when I was mad at her. But right now, I was totally pissed off.

I rolled my eyes and walked out of the store. I didn't feel like explaining it to Zena, India, or anyone else. And I didn't feel like shopping anymore.

I just wanted to get something to eat.

"So you didn't get the jeans?" Diamond asked as if she couldn't believe it.

"Don't ask her that unless you want to get your feelings hurt," India said as she stuffed a piece of avocado from her salad into her mouth.

I rolled my eyes at both of them, but I wasn't mad. I was just glad that we had finally stopped to get something to eat. This was supposed to be a famous restaurant—the News Café—and it was great, because we got to sit outside, right across from the beach.

So I was feeling good—until Diamond repeated her question.

"What's up with the jeans?" she asked.

Rolling my eyes should have been enough. But this was Diamond's world; we were only invited to live in it, and if she wanted to talk, we talked.

I sighed, but before I could say anything, Diamond said, "Oh, I get it; they were too expensive, huh?" She popped a French fry in her mouth. "You should've just told Zena. That's what I did. The Judge paid for mine 'cause I wasn't about to spend any of my money."

India shook her head. "You better leave it alone, Diamond."

Veronique frowned. "Would someone tell *me* what's going on?"

I put down my fork. There was no way this was going to stop unless I talked. "I saw a pair of jeans—"

"Not some ordinary jeans," Diamond said, waving a French fry in the air.

"A pair of jeans that cost over two hundred dollars," I said.

"Dang! But everything down here seems to be expensive," Veronique said. "So you didn't get them?"

"No," I shook my head.

Then India said, "She could've gotten them, though, because Zena said she would pay for them, but Aaliyah said no."

Together, Diamond and Veronique said, "What?" and looked at me like I had lost my mind.

Diamond said, "Why wouldn't you let her buy them?"

I tried to explain that I didn't want Zena to think I only wanted her money, but none of my girls were hearing it.

"She's your mother," India said. "You guys are fine now, and she wants to buy you nice things."

"Yeah," Diamond said. "You'd better let her spend her money on you now before we win this contest. Then all of

167

them"—she pointed to the table across from us where our mothers sat—"will be expecting us to buy stuff for them."

We all laughed with Diamond at that one, but I wasn't about to change my mind.

Veronique said, "Don't let my mom offer to buy me a thing. I'm taking it! I don't care what it is—a pack of gum? It's mine!"

We laughed again; then a couple of really tall girls walked by our table and Diamond forgot about me. She went straight into her expert mode.

"You see those girls?" She was supposed to be whispering, but she was talking so loud, I was surprised the girls didn't turn around and stare her down. Diamond said, "They're models for sure. Did you know that South Beach is the model-shoot capital of the world?"

I frowned. "I thought Paris was."

Diamond waved her hand like what I said wasn't important. "Well, maybe not of the world, but South Beach is definitely the United States capital."

I didn't know if she was right or wrong. I was just glad that she had changed the subject and was now lecturing us on all things South Beach—including telling us that we just had to go by Gianni Versace's house, which was just a couple of blocks from where we were. "It's a big tourist attraction," she continued, being the know-it-all.

I didn't say anything, but I wasn't going there. Like anyone would want to see where that man got shot!

But whatever. At least Diamond wasn't talking about me and Zena. And Zena's money. 'Cause no matter what, I would never be able to get my girls to get it—they would never understand that I didn't want anything else from Zena. All I wanted from her, I already had.

I looked over at the table where she was sitting with

Ms. Elizabeth, Ms. Tova, and Ms. Lena. Then, as if she knew I was looking, she turned around, smiled, and waved. I waved back.

Yup, I already had everything that I wanted.

I had my mother.

Chapter 25

We had all the moves.

The Three Ys Men were poppin' and lockin' around us on this stage, and everyone in that convention center was on their feet. I felt like we had already won the contest, because with the band backing us up and the bigger stage, it felt like we were performing in a real concert.

The only thing was that there was so much cheering going on, I just hoped that the audience—and the judges—could hear us singing.

But as I sang my last part, I wasn't too worried. Zena had told us that the whole act was the most important thing in this part of the competition. And between the Divine Divas and the Three Ys Men, we were giving them a straight-up act!

We held that last note as long as we could, but the crowd was already stomping and cheering. And we started cheering, too—the moment we ran off the stage.

We had nailed it!

"Man, that was better than New York!" Arjay high-fived Riley.

"You know it, son," Troy said.

We were still congratulating each other when Sybil dragged us all back to our waiting room. I was thinking that when we got in there we would see Pastor Ford and my dad, and all the other people who'd come down to Florida from Hope Chapel. But when we got back there, the room was empty.

I frowned—there was no cake, no sodas, no nothing like the celebrations we usually had.

But it seemed like I was the only one who noticed, because my girls and the guys were still talking and laughing.

Diamond said, "We were so fierce!"

I had to agree with my girl. I mean, we always got a standing ovation, but I didn't remember people cheering for us like that in any of the other cities. And none of the other groups that sang tonight made the crowd go crazy the way it did for us. Yeah, Diamond was right—we were fierce.

Sybil agreed, "You guys were all great." At least that's what she said, but her face didn't match her words. She wasn't smiling—she was serious.

Then I remembered . . . we had another song to sing. The big one. With Zena.

And this time we wouldn't have the Three Ys Men backing us up. It would be just us.

But we had Zena—shouldn't that be enough?

"Here," Sybil said, handing us water bottles. "Drink up, rest your throats. You only have about ten minutes."

She gave us a look that said, Don't play, and then she left us alone.

Just a few minutes ago, we were all happy. But now, as I looked around at my girls, we were as serious as Sybil—and more nervous than I think we'd ever been before.

"Okay," Arjay said, clapping his hands, like he knew we needed a pep talk. "You girls are 'bout to go out there and shut this whole thing down, right?" He put his arms around Veronique and Diamond.

"That's what I thought before," Veronique said. I don't think I had ever heard her talk so softly. "But why did Sybil seem so nervous?"

Riley said, "She didn't seem nervous to me," but the way he said it, I could tell he was lying. He was just trying to make us feel better.

"Maybe she thinks it'll be harder singing with Zena," India said. My BFFL sounded like she was more than nervous—she sounded straight-up scared.

Even Diamond didn't have her usual totally confident look.

"Okay, now this is crazy. Y'all need to chill," Troy said. "You know you're gonna bring it home. Just stop talking about it and be about it. Get your heads together and go out there and make it happen!"

Whoa! Now that was a pep talk.

I took a deep breath. "Yeah," I said.

"Yeah," my girls said after me.

It was like Troy had slapped us straight. What had we been thinking? I mean, we had practiced with Zena a thousand times—we couldn't be any more ready.

And sure, the other groups had Yolanda Adams and Faith Evans and Patti LaBelle. But we had Zena—the only one so famous she just had one name.

For about five minutes, we all stayed quiet. My girls and I fixed our makeup, and, in our heads, we went over the song. The guys sat on the other side of the room, whispering to each other and watching us. I could feel Troy looking at me. And for some reason, that made me feel even better.

Then Zena walked in the room.

She was wearing a long black sequined gown that matched the short dresses we had on. And with her hair all out and her makeup done, she looked beautiful to me. Like a superstar.

"Ladies." She spoke so softly and so calmly. As if she had done this a million times before.

I guess she had.

She walked to the center of the room and held her hands out. I took one of her hands, and Diamond took the other. Then, all of us—including the guys—stood in a circle. And Zena prayed for us.

When she finished, Troy reached over and hugged me. When he said, "You got this," I had to laugh. All this time, he'd been telling me, "I got you." I guess it was time for me to step up and take care of myself—at least through this song.

Slowly, Zena led us out of the room. As we moved to the stage, I wondered if my girls were thinking what I was. This was going to be our last song; no matter what went down to-night, this would be the last time we'd be competing in the Glory 2 God Teen Talent Search.

I couldn't believe it. We had come such a long way since we first started in September. We'd gone from Los Angeles to San Francisco, then to New York. We'd been through every-thing from Diamond's parents almost keeping her out of the group, to India's stomach rupturing, then Veronique almost being kidnapped. We'd gone from just singing on our own to having the guys dance with us.

And there was my drama with Zena.

But we were still here. In the last city, getting ready to sing the last song. If we made this happen, we would be on our way to being stars. Maybe even superstars like Zena.

"Ladies and gentlemen," I heard the announcer say, "Zena and the Divine Divas!"

We held hands as we walked onto the stage. Jackie was already sitting at the keyboard, and she smiled, trying to give us some confidence. But it wasn't until Zena looked at me and nodded that I felt better—it was then that I knew we were gonna do the darn thing. Win or lose.

Zena started, "I will lift up my eyes. . . ."

I swayed behind her, in step with Diamond, India, and Veronique. Then Diamond went forward, and just like in practice, she tore it up. India did, too. And Veronique . . . she just did what she do—she broke it down.

My hands were shaking when I stepped up for my turn; I took a deep breath, but then Zena stepped away from her stool.

I frowned—I didn't have any idea what she was doing. She took my hand and said, "Ladies and gentlemen, this is my daughter, Aaliyah Reid."

People in the audience started to whisper, but no one was more surprised than me. Then they started clapping, but I didn't know what to do because we had kinda gotten off track. Then Zena nodded, squeezed my hand, and we started singing our part. We held hands through our whole duet.

I knew Zena and I rocked it, because people stood to their feet and starting swaying. And lifting their hands in the air. They weren't clapping like before—it was more like the way when people stood in church, when they got happy just hearing the choir sing.

After my part, my girls stepped forward and we sang the next chorus together. We kept looking at each other, and there were tears in all of our eyes. I knew they were thinking what I was—that good or bad, this was the end.

And so at the end of the song, we all held that last note as if we didn't want to ever let go.

For a couple of seconds it was so quiet. And then the

applause began, sounding just like thunder the way the audience clapped their hands and stomped their feet.

We stayed right there on that stage, hugging and kissing and crying together.

When Zena came and hugged me, that's when I cried the most.

She leaned back and wiped the tears from my face with her fingers. "You sang beautifully, baby."

I hugged her again and whispered in her ear, "Thanks, Mom."

Chapter 26

This was worse than any of the times before.

I couldn't take it. Standing on this stage, under all of these hot lights, waiting—it was just too much for me.

The judges had made their decision—they'd told us that five minutes ago. So what was taking them so long to tell us? Didn't they know that I had passed out before because of stress?

I really wished Zena could be with me. But they just wanted the competing groups on the stage. At least the Three Ys Men were allowed; that was a good thing, because Troy was standing next to me—so if I fainted, he would be right there to make sure I didn't hit the floor.

I looked over at Diamond and India and Veronique. They were standing as still as statues, looking as scared as I was. Somebody needed to call the police on Mr. Roberto and those judges. Nobody should be allowed to treat teenagers like this, making us wait, keeping us in suspense. I felt like a hostage; my heart couldn't take it.

Finally, Mr. Roberto walked slowly up to the stage. And then he smiled at the first group, but he didn't even look at us. My heart started doing that fast-beating thing again.

Oh, no, I thought. *We lost.*

I had to start taking deep breaths. And then I had to remember that I hadn't really wanted to be in the Divine Divas in the first place. I was going to Harvard in two years—remember? I was going to be a nuclear physicist—right? So it didn't matter what went down here tonight.

Except—it did matter! I wanted to win. I wanted to be part of the Divine Divas and get this recording contract. I wanted to cut a CD.

Truth—I wanted to sing, just like my mother.

Mr. Roberto started talking. "When we started this competition, we didn't expect to find such talent." He turned around and looked at all of us. "I'm telling you, every single last one of you could be signed to a contract tonight and I know you would all be successful."

That was a perfect idea! They should sign all of us and then we wouldn't have to go through all of this.

Then he said, "But there can only be one winner." He took a breath. "It was a tough, tough decision. But the winners of the Glory 2 God Teen Talent Search are . . ."

I closed my eyes, and Troy squeezed my hand. He whispered, "I got you. . . ." right before Mr. Roberto said, "The winners are the Divine Divas!"

I heard our name, but it took a moment for our name to get to my brain. Then three things happened: Diamond did her Diamond screech thing, Troy lifted me off the ground and hugged me, and Zena ran from behind the curtains and kissed me.

The Divine Divas had won!

All of a sudden, the stage was crowded with all the people from Hope Chapel. It was hard to see everybody 'cause my eyes were filled to the top with tears. I did know my dad, though, when he hugged me and kissed me and told me over and over how proud he was of me.

And Pastor Ford . . . wow! I had never seen her cry before—but the way she was bawling, she was the biggest baby on the stage.

It took some time before Mr. Roberto got us all to kinda calm down, because he said there were some other things he wanted to say. I thought he was gonna make the Hope Chapel people get off the stage, but it was a good thing that he didn't. It would've taken at least an hour to move all of them.

So while Diamond, India, Veronique, and I stood in the middle of a big ole circle, Mr. Roberto explained to us and to the audience that we would begin working on the release of our first single right away and that people would be able to buy it before the end of the year.

Before the end of the year!

Oh, my God! I was gonna be a star in less than six months. And then I had to laugh at myself. I was starting to sound like Diamond.

As soon as Mr. Roberto finished talking, I finally got the chance to hug my girls. First Diamond, who I really did love, even though she got on all of my nerves most of the time. Then, India, the best and sweetest BFFL in the whole world. Next, I hugged Veronique, my soul sistah, who taught me so much about keepin' it real.

My girls. My sisters. I said, "I love you guys."

"We love you, too," they said together.

Inside the circle, we put our hands together, one on top of the other like the guys did on the football and basketball teams. And then we let out a big cheer.

"The Divine Divas!" we shouted.

We were the winners—straight-up!

Readers Group Guide

Summary

Best friends Diamond, India, Veronique, and Aaliyah are fifteen-year-old high school sophomores who make up the singing group The Divine Divas. When The Divas are selected to participate in a nationwide gospel talent search that is looking for the next great teen singing stars, Aaliyah reluctantly goes along with the group. Even though she is more focused on going to college to become a nuclear physicist than on becoming a singing star, her loyalty to her friends wins out over her personal desire. When the girls qualify for the finals, they discover that the talent search has set them up with a celebrity mentor who will perform with them. The rest of the group is thrilled to discover that their mentor will be Zena, the pop singing sensation and worldwide star. Aaliyah is not quite as excited, because what the rest of the group doesn't know is that Zena is Aaliyah's mother, who Aaliyah claimed was dead after she left her family to pursue her career. But what begins as the biggest challenge that Aaliyah has ever faced may just turn out to be a blessing in disguise for both Aaliyah and Zena.

Questions for Discussion

1. Why do you think that Aaliyah told her best friends that her mother was dead, rather than the truth that she had left her and her father for a career? Even if she didn't tell the entire group, why didn't she tell India, who is her BFFL?

2. With all of the excitement that surrounds Zena, especially when everyone discovers that she is Aaliyah's mother, why doesn't Aaliyah enjoy having a superstar mother more? Would you enjoy it if your mother were a world-famous singer?

3. Why do you think Aaliyah doesn't want to start a new relationship with Zena when she returns?

4. Why does Zena decide that now is the time to reappear in Aaliyah's life? What is her motivation, and why now, when Aaliyah is turning sixteen?

5. When Aaliyah is trying to get Zena to stop being the celebrity mentor for The Divine Divas, why does her father refuse to help her make Zena quit the competition?

6. Aaliyah talks about "the Big S" for "suck it up." What do

you think are some of the lessons that she learns from doing things that she doesn't want to do? How do you think her faith in God helps her?

7. Pastor Ford tells Aaliyah that this is an opportunity for her. In what ways do you think that this is true? What are her new opportunities?

8. Of all of Aaliyah's friends, Diamond has the strongest "star-struck" reaction to Zena, which at times annoys Aaliyah. Do you think Diamond's reaction is selfish? Is Aaliyah's reaction to Diamond fair?

9. When Zena confesses to Aaliyah that she hates herself for leaving, Aaliyah admits to herself that she feels slightly bad. Why?

10. Even though Aaliyah told everyone her mother was dead, she bought Mother's Day cards for Zena and kept them. Why do you think she did this?

11. Why do you think that Aaliyah is embarrassed by Zena's luxurious lifestyle—the limousines, the outfits, etc.?

12. Aaliyah's father tells her that "there were blessings in every situation." What blessings does Aaliyah discover in hers?

13. Even though she initially declines it, Aaliyah eventually accepts the Range Rover that Zena buys her for her birthday. Why? Why, after accepting the Range Rover, does she then decline when Zena wants to purchase the expensive jeans for her?

14. When Zena invites Aaliyah to brunch, she doesn't want to go alone and brings Troy along. Why is she still uncomfortable being alone with Zena?

15. On some level, do you feel Aaliyah has really loved Zena all along and just hasn't realized it?

Enhancing Your
Book Club Discussion

1. Have a contest among your friends and fellow book club members. Set a time limit and see how many all-girl singing groups each of you can name. Decide on a prize, and whoever names the most groups wins.

2. There are various resources online for aspiring singers and songwriters. As part of your discussion, work with your friends and book club members to write your own song on a subject that is important to all of you.

3. Visit iTunes, Amazon, or your favorite online music store and create a playlist that you think fits the theme of the book and the personality of Aaliyah. If you come up with something great, make playlists for Diamond, India, and Veronique as well.

4. As one of the themes of *Aaliyah* is motherhood, ask your mother for one of her favorite recipes and then make it for the rest of the group.

Visit SimonandSchuster.com for an exclusive interview with Victoria Christopher Murray.

Don't miss the first Divine Divas adventure

The Divas: Diamond

Available from Pocket Books

Turn the page for a preview of *Diamond*. . . .

1

"We're gonna be so paid!"

I waved my magazine in the air and dumped my messenger bag onto the lunch table. I waited for my crew to say something, but not one of them even looked at me.

"Hello? Anybody home?"

India stuffed half a hot dog into her mouth. "I heard you."

"So, if you heard me, why aren't you excited?" But I wasn't just talking to India. I wondered what was wrong with Veronique and Aaliyah, too.

"Because," Aaliyah began, not taking her eyes away from whatever book she was reading, "you're *always* excited about something, Diamond."

"And what's wrong with that?" I asked. "I'm fifteen and fine! I'm supposed to be excited."

Veronique unplugged one of the earplugs from the MP3 player we'd given her for her birthday. "You are so the drama queen."

"Whatever, whatever. Call me what you want; I'm going to

be a paid drama queen. And I'm gonna let y'all ride because I love you and I'm special like that."

Veronique tried not to grin, but I knew she was feelin' me. She pushed her earplug in place and lay back on the bench.

When no one said anything else, I said, "Don't you want to know how I'm gonna make you rich?"

"Diamond," India said, now chomping on French fries, "you're already rich."

"Nuh-huh. My parents have money, but they've told me and my brother over and over that it's their money, not ours." I shrugged. "But it doesn't matter 'cause in less than a year, the cash will be flowin' my way."

Veronique sat up. "Okay, I'll bite. What's up?"

One down. But I still had to stare at India like she'd stolen something before she paid me more attention than she did her French fries. And then, we all had to give Aaliyah the evil eye before she—with a sigh—half-closed her book.

With their eyes on me now, I snapped the magazine open to the centerfold. "Peep this!"

India, Veronique, and Aaliyah stared at the pages that announced the gospel talent search, but then just as quickly, India tossed a handful of French fries into her mouth, Veronique stuffed her ears with the plugs again, and Aaliyah went back to her book as if she'd never stopped reading.

I could not believe them. I loved my crew like they were my own sisters. In fact, we always said we were sisters, since none of us had any biological sisters. But today I wanted to give them all back to their mothers.

"What are you guys doing?" I waited a moment. When no one answered me, I bounced on top of the bench even though I had rolled up my skirt so that it would look like a mini. "Hello!" I yelled. "Does anyone besides me want to be a star?"

There were plenty of cackles from everyone else in the school yard, but nothing from my crew.

Finally, Veronique said, "You're the one who wants to be a star, my sistah."

"Well, yeah," I said, wondering why she was taking the time to state the obvious. "Because I was born to be one. And we live in L.A. We're supposed to be stars."

"I don't want to be one." India wrinkled her nose like she smelled something nasty.

"Me neither," Veronique and Aaliyah piped in.

"That's un-American," I said. "But this is about more than just being a star." I paused, letting the drama build. "What if I told you we were about to be paid a million dollars?"

That made Veronique take both plugs from her ears. "A million dollars? Tell me more, my sistah."

"Actually, it's more like two hundred and fifty thousand."

Aaliyah lifted her eyes from her book just long enough to say, "That's a long way from a million."

I rolled my eyes. Leave it to the analytical one to take my words literally. Still, I said, "Not by much. And anyway, that's just the start. When we win this contest, we'll get phat contracts and we'll certainly have a million dollars then. Probably more."

"Go for it," Aaliyah said.

I rolled my eyes toward heaven and asked the Lord to help me. "You're supposed to be the smart one. Didn't you read that this is a group competition?"

"So, that's what this is about," India said. "You need a group; you need us." She shook her head. "And I thought you were telling us about this because you loved us."

"Love you, I do. But on the real, I need you." I paused, lifted the magazine, and began reading, "Glory 2 God Productions is the latest record label to take advantage of the

American Idol phenomenon. Announcing their own talent show, G2G president Roberto Hamilton said, 'We're looking for fresh talent with hip-hop flavor, but with the heart and love for the Lord. We're excited about the possibilities. Our plan is to make the winning group superstars.'" I slammed the magazine shut. "They are obviously talking about us."

"We're not a group," Veronique said.

Inside, I moaned. "Not yet. But if you guys would pay attention and start dreaming this dream with me, we'd have a group in"—I looked at my watch—"how long will it take for us to come up with a name?" When no one answered, I whined, "Come on."

Veronique nodded her head slowly, as if she'd had a little peek into my dream. I knew I could count on her. Even though I considered India and Aaliyah my best friends, too, I was closest to Vee, which was what we called her. Veronique was quite different from me; she was different from all of us. With her wild, bronze-colored fro, the little gold stud in her nose, and wooden and beaded bangles up and down her arm, she looked like she was some kind of flower child from the sixties. I think she got her style from her mom. It was kind of old-fashioned to me, but I loved Veronique anyway. And I loved her even more right about now.

I clapped my hands. "So, you're in?"

Veronique said, "I didn't say that. I need to know more."

I sighed as India and Aaliyah looked at me like they agreed with Veronique. What more did they possibly need? Sometimes I wondered how we all became friends, because I was so far ahead of them it wasn't even funny. I believed in dreams that they hadn't even begun to imagine. But I stayed with them because India, Veronique, and Aaliyah needed me. India needed me to help her with her self-confidence, Veronique needed me to show her life's possibilities, and Aaliyah needed me . . . well,

I wasn't sure what Aaliyah needed from me because she always acted like she didn't need anybody. But I loved them all.

I said, "Okay, what else do you need to know besides the fact that Glory 2 God Productions is doing a national talent search to discover us?"

"Are we old enough to enter?" India asked as she dumped her empty food containers into the trash.

"This is a teen competition, so you have to be between the ages of thirteen and eighteen. I guess nineteen is too close to twenty. And after that, all we need is to be sponsored by our church."

"Sponsored? What does that mean?" Aaliyah asked.

"I don't know, but whatever it is, Pastor Ford will do it for us."

"Are you sure?" Veronique asked. "Pastor's never heard us sing."

"What are you talking about? We sing in church every month."

Aaliyah said, "You want to enter the entire choir in this contest?"

I looked at Aaliyah wide-eyed. There was no doubt she was the brains; Aaliyah had never received anything less than an A since elementary school. But sometimes she acted like her brain went on vacation. "Of course I'm not talking about the entire choir. I'm talking about just us. If we can sing in the choir, why can't we form our own little group?" When they said nothing, I added, "Okay, let me break this down to you like you're two-year-olds: the four of us form a group, go to church, get sponsored, send in the applications, begin practicing, sing some songs, do some steps, win . . . and then get the big bucks."

"I like that big bucks part," Veronique said.

"So, you're in?" I asked.

India, Veronique, and Aaliyah looked at each other, and inside, I prayed, *Please, God, let my crew have some sense*.

Slowly, India and Veronique nodded. But Aaliyah held out her hand. I tossed her the magazine, then watched her look over the article.

"This says that the participants are responsible for their own expenses. . . ."

"Expenses?" Veronique frowned.

Aaliyah continued, "All travel, lodging, and any expenses associated with the contest will be the responsibility of the applicants."

"So, hold up." Veronique stopped Aaliyah. "How much money are they talking about?"

"According to this," Aaliyah paused and read some more, "if we win in Los Angeles, we'd have to pay our way to San Francisco. Then to . . ."

Veronique shook her head. "I can't afford to be in this contest."

I was about to burst with frustration. "Why're you worrying about the money right now? Let's just form the group. If we're serious, you know my parents will cover everything."

"No way," Veronique said, lying back down on the bench. "My mother is not about to spend money she doesn't have. At least that's what she's always telling me."

"I said don't worry about the money."

"We have to think about how much this will cost. If we win this, like you say, we'd have to go all the way to . . . ," Aaliyah said as she looked down at the magazine, "New York and Miami."

Veronique bolted up from the bench. "New York? When would we go to New York?"

I guess somehow money wasn't a problem for her now.

"That's where the semifinals are going to be," Aaliyah said.

"I always wanted to go to New York." Veronique bit her lip, then said to India and Aaliyah, "Maybe we should talk to Pastor Ford and see what she thinks."

"Okay, I'm willing to start there." I was doing everything I could to hold in my excitement. "So, are y'all ready to roll with me?" I held out my hand, and after a couple of moments, Veronique gave me a high five. Then, India. And although I could tell she wasn't really feeling this, Aaliyah finally did the same.

"You know singing ain't my thing," Aaliyah pouted. "But y'all my sisters, so when you roll, I roll."

I grinned. None of them were as excited as I was, but all they needed was a little time. India, Veronique, and Aaliyah had no idea how blessed they were to have me. I was on my way to making us all stars!